IGNITING THE WITCH

WILDE WITCHES - PREQUEL

ERIN RICHARDS

Midnight Muse
PUBLISHING

IGNITING THE WITCH
Erin Richards

Digital ISBN: 978-1943800216
Print ISBN: 978-1943800223

Cover Designer: Book Cover Artistry by Heather Hamilton-Senter

PRAISE FOR
ERIN RICHARDS' BOOKS

"I loved this book [*Chasing Shadows*] and it never faltered from its action and suspense." ~*Night Owl Reviews (NOR 5-Star Top Pick)*

"*Stealing Twilight* by Erin Richards is completely enthralling with its addicting characters, unique plot, and satisfying ending." ~*Amazon 5-Star Review*

"*Seducing Darkness* is fast-paced and action-packed. It is well-written with vivid imagery that allowed me to get lost in the story. It offers drama, intrigue, and romance with a hint of humor that kept me entertained throughout." ~*Amazon 5-Star Review*

"Full of adventure, romance and two wonderfully heroic characters. The descriptions of the island are beautiful and the passion between Morgan and Ryan leaves you turning the pages to see if they can finally come together. A great book [*Wicked Paradise*]." ~*5-Stars, Paranormal Romance Guild*

"Perfect for fans of Julie Kagawa & Alyssa Rose Ivy. Loved this book [*Forbidden Thirteen*]! The plot was unique in a genre where everything has been done before. Just the perfect balance of action, supernatural and hot romance. Bring on book 2!" ~*5-Star Amazon Review*

BOOKS BY
ERIN RICHARDS

Psychic Justice Series
Chasing Shadows, Book 1
Twilight Rising, Book 2
Stealing Twilight, Book 3
Seducing Darkness, Book 4
Tempting Midnight, Book 5

Forbidden Legacy Series
Forbidden Thirteen, Book 1

Wilde Witches Series
Igniting the Witch, Prequel
Black Magic Rising, Book 1
Black Warlocks Prowling, Book 2
Black Curses Brewing, Book 3

Wicked Paradise

Young Adult
Vigilante Nights
Dragonfly Nightmare
Bittersweet Wreckage

See updated book list at:
www.erinrichards.com/booklist.htm

IGNITING THE WITCH

Chapter 1

The back of Sage's neck prickled as she stumbled through the covenstead woods. Her slippery ankle boots skid on the dew-covered path, and she slowed down before she face-planted herself. Dim and misty pre-dawn light shrouded the forest, giving nothing away, but she could feel the eyes of something watching her. Low landscape lights and her phone flashlight guided her toward the house, and she couldn't walk fast enough to reach it.

Owls hooting in the towering evergreens abruptly stopped. In response, her owl familiars churned over her skin beneath her blouse. The ink of their tattoo forms tickled her already prickling flesh. More than the hushed forest owls gave her familiars the heebie-jeebies. An ethereal purple glow filtered through the trees and muted the stars overhead, creating an eerie environment that didn't help.

Powerful magic hit her senses. Elemental fire and air. Out of place on the off-limits walkway, but not threatening. Yet. Her familiars caught wind of the crackling magic and tiny flying embers. They swooshed over her skin, preparing to launch off her in protection mode. Sage halted on the path she'd traveled since she'd learned to walk. Wood smoke filtered through the early summer air. The faint brackish scent of the Pacific Ocean also tinged the air, destined to drive the smoke away.

"Gwyneira," she berated her main familiar, trying to halt their roaming over her already sensitive chest. Fat chance. Their apprehensive roving continued driving her nuts. She didn't need crazy on top of her thundering headache. One too many tequila shots on the first night of the California covens' Summer Solstice festival. Thank the goddess, she'd only sexed it up with one warlock, though eight had vied for her attention. More than one would've ruined her for the day, for sure.

The warlock she'd chosen to spend the night with had fallen asleep the minute he came inside her, and she'd slipped from his tent without waking him. Joshua's single-minded focus did nothing for her in the arousal department. Maybe the reason he was an unattached warlock. Damn, she needed a good lay with a man who knew how to please a woman. Maybe she'd have better luck tonight.

And her brain had a mind of its own when she needed to concentrate on the magic surrounding her. *Focus, Sage!*

The foreign magic didn't hurt or impede her, but it raised red flags. A hollow, sparking fireball rolled off her fingers and danced on her open right palm. She used her left hand to draw a ring of witch-air to splinter the magic surrounding her. The unknown fire magic scattered into embers and reformed, also killing the landscape lights.

"Crap on a cracker." Sage flashed her phone light around her to illuminate the nearby trees and pea gravel path. "Who's there?" She spun in a circle, drilling her sight into the gray dawn, made darker by the woods. "Show yourself. Now," she demanded. After all, she owned the land. She ruled the California region and the coven members who'd arrived on the covenstead yesterday. By tomorrow, she'd become the youngest High Priestess of the entire western witchworld, following in her deceased mother's footsteps. A position held by a Wilde witch for over a century. Threats to her were a witch-style jail sentence!

Ire trekked up her spine in a cold ripple. "Either reveal yourself or take a hike off my land. You're no longer welcome at the solstice gathering."

The unknown witch-fire sizzled around her fireball, hovering over her palm. She sniffed the foreign fire to discern the source. No dice in the familiarity department. It touched her hand for a second before her witch-water doused and iced the burn.

Freaking Zelda Helwig. The bane of my coven's existence. "Zelda. I know it's you. What do you want? If you're trying to scare me, you're shit out of luck. Don't forget who you're screwing with. We've crawled this road before. Didn't end well for the Helwigs." The High Priestess of the Scotts Valley coven held a distinct edge to her witch-fire, and her fire always shifted to teal blue when it touched skin. Zelda knew how to disguise her magic, the reason Sage let it touch her, despite the burn to her hand. Zelda also possessed a rare double element with witch-air, and both elements dangled in the air. Silence greeted her.

"You're on report to the Council. See you on the flipside, *Zelda*." Sage slogged down the path toward the house, increasing her pace, the sky lightening to a paler gray through the treetops. Passing by several dead landscape lights, she tripped in a rut and collapsed on her butt.

"Goddess, save me." She massaged her rear, rubbed her aching head. Hangover cotton stuffed her mouth. She'd kill for a toothbrush and a bottle of aspirin. And a long, hot shower.

Her familiars stopped moving, their tattoo bodies quivering in awareness on her skin. Crashes through the bushes to her right stilled her movements. Her familiars scurried up to Sage's shoulder and launched off her. They shifted into their natural form, and threads of glowing magic dangled from their talons.

Ignoring the literal pain in her ass, Sage vaulted up to her feet. Fireballs formed on both palms. A low-throated snarling joined the rustling in the brush. Too dark and too hungover to find her way home by walking backward to watch her back, Sage stood her ground. The shuffling moved from her left to her right, then crashed through the underbrush toward her. She tossed fireballs toward the sounds, and the balls hit the drought-stricken forest floor. Flames flared up, and she sprinkled witch-water to douse the fire before she ignited the entire mountainside. Gwyneira flew in a circle to encapsulate whatever threatened her in threads of witch-air. No such luck. The invisible animals escaped her familiar's magic. Growling and snarling arose to her other side, then behind her, circling her, but not approaching. Near enough to drive more chills up her spine.

Peering into the dim forest, she let her eyes adjust to search for any signs of wildlife or other life. The Wilde property was crawling with people in tents and cabins for the solstice festival. The presence of the witches and their entourages should've driven all the natural wildlife farther into the depths of the mountains. Which meant these little shits were no ordinary animals.

"Your ass is grass now," Sage yelled and tossed three more fireballs, chased them with a sprinkle of witch-water. No need to add forest fire to the overflowing Blame-it-on-Sage card.

"Who's there?" She strengthened her wobbly voice to hide her fear. "I swear to the goddess, if you don't call off your familiars, I'm gonna go *loco* on you. And you don't want to experience my kind of crazy." Was it a witch or a warlock she'd shunned last night? Plenty of enemies or naysayers had a bull's-eye on Sage's forehead, jealous of her position, her power, her standing in the witchworld at only twenty-four years old. *Well, hell, it's not like I offed my mother just to steal her crown.*

A growling and snarling animal approached, soon joined by several more, glamoured by an invisibility spell. The air wavered and the forest floor debris ruffled. They snarled and snapped as if they wanted to eat her alive. Sage spun her left fingers in the air, invoking a protection bubble of witch-air. Hard to tell if they were foxes or bobcats, or something equally frightening. Not like she knew the sounds the forest animals or all the familiars in the world made.

She wracked her hungover brain to recall Zelda's familiar. A bobcat? Gray fox? Both remained prevalent in the hills of the Helwig covenstead in Scotts Valley up the highway, which shared the same mountain range as the Wilde coven.

"Sage Wilde," a hoarse, unrecognizable voice floated out on a gust of wind. Definitely female.

"What do you want?" she demanded, safe in her

warded bubble. The beasts on the ground held their positions, which meant they definitely were familiars. A real animal could infiltrate a protection circle. Not so much a familiar.

"You don't deserve the High Priestess role of California, let alone the entire western region."

"Stop the world so I can jump off." Sage tipped her head back to face the pinkening sky. Same old, same old. "Why? Because every horny warlock under the sun wants me? Or 'cause I can drink myself to oblivion and live to tell about it? Because I'm wild, loose, inexperienced, and *young*." Sarcasm dripped from her tone. She'd heard the ridiculous litany of complaints from a myriad of sources since her mother and father wound up dead at the bottom of a canyon in the Lake Tahoe Mountains. A drunk driver had forced their car to career over a cliff last year. Big freaking deal if she wanted to enjoy her twenties before real life took a spin at her.

A flaming arrow pierced her protective bubble, missing her right shoulder by a skosh. A real flaming arrow, not magical. Rubbing her shoulder, she ducked to the ground, scrambled off the path into a thicket of bushes amid a cedar grove. Shit just got real. She lugged her protection circle with her, and the gaggle of snarling invisible animals followed, keeping their three-foot distance. Once they fenced her in again, their tails swished dead leaves, twigs, and evergreen needles on the forest floor, which eclipsed the taut silence.

Sage eased her cell phone out of the back pocket of her skin-tight denim skirt and tapped her nine-one-one.

Her sole bonded warlock answered. "Ready for me to come get you?" He yawned loud enough to wake the dead.

"Ricky. Listen. I'm on the north path leading from the meadow. Someone's attacking me. Real arrows, actual threats. A witch."

Rustling sounds accompanied Ricky's stern voice. "On my way. Keep the line open. Can't you use magic?"

"I'm in a protective circle, but magic won't do spit against flaming arrows. I'd rather not use wind magic to force them away and risk setting the forest on fire. Can't see the glamoured familiars, and they've surrounded me."

"Move closer to the house in the protective ward."

"Too dangerous with all the people here for the festival. I need to ground my circle here. Any hole in my ward can trigger these gremlins to attack."

"I knew this was a bad idea," he groused. "I'm snagging the first witches I see. On the way. Here, talk to your sister."

"Hey," her middle sister, Aspen, chirped into the phone.

"I've had enough of today already. We're in a no-magic period. Festivals are supposed to be safe zones for everyone to set aside their beefs for three days." She spoke louder for her stalker to hear her ranting.

"Did a stupid rock hit you on the way to your orgy?" Aspen chortled. "Ya think the Helwigs and their minions care one wit about rules?"

A flush of annoyance stole up Sage's chest. "Shut up." She knew better. But alcohol and sex spoke a unique language.

"Sage, honey." Concern rode her aunt Jessica's voice. "Are you safe?"

"Safe as can be." Another flaming arrow hit the ground at her feet, and she scurried behind a cedar tree. She swished her hand like a hose nozzle and doused the fire.

A telltale ache formed behind her eyes. Gritty eyeballs and blurry vision chased the pain. *What the holy goddess?* Her buried aether magic hadn't surfaced in years. Such powerful magic, she never used it, nor ever controlled it. Why now?

"Son of a witch's tit. Gotta jam." She hung up and wedged the phone in her pocket. Spine stiff, she stood and readied fireballs on her palms. Using her witch-air, she tossed the fireballs at the ground where her four-legged stalkers waited. Witch-water followed to extinguish any flames.

She uttered a silent spell to control the flames and launched more balls of fire. They sizzled to the ground, and embers showered the air. Dirt, dried leaves, and twigs pinged her shield. Flames threatened to engulf the creatures, and they yelped an ear-piercing sound. They fled, their screeches fading into the depths of the woods. A fire spread across the dry forest floor, consuming a small ribbon of land, the heat exacerbating the natural heat of her body. She raised her hands, ready to use her witch-water to extinguish the flames. But to her surprise and joy, the fire died down on its own, leaving nothing but ash and smoke. Her silent incantation to douse the flames reverberated in the air. A spell always just out of her reach. Knots untied in her shoulders, and she returned to the path. Why now had her rare aether magic emerged and aided her witch-fire?

The unseen witch uttered her final say, "You won't see me coming next time. I won't hold back either." The words dissipated in the misty morning air, floating toward the Pacific Ocean.

The threat drove shivers down Sage's spine. She hiked through a puff of smoke and raised witch-air to dispel it. Fear and uncertainty lingered in her mind. She'd taken her security for granted. Took life for granted. The incident was the proverbial straw that broke the camel's back. The time had arrived to prove to the witchworld that she was a smart, capable adult, not a silly, irresponsible party animal. Maybe then they'd respect her magic. Respect her, period.

Chapter 2

Footsteps approached from the direction of the house. Sage readied her witch-fire for blast off, but the gloomy dawn revealed Ricky, Aspen, and Jessica. Cell phone flashlights lit the gravel pathway and bounced up. Their eyes glommed onto her, radiating a mixture of curiosity and concern.

"Are you okay?" asked Jessica, her mother's twin sister. They weren't identical twins, which helped smother her grief every time she looked at Jessica. Jessica had already donned her ubiquitous fashionable jeans and a loose, shimmery silk blouse. A light layer of makeup on her youthful face accented her short-layered brunette hair, styled for the day. Way too early for Sage.

The sun emerged above the distant horizon, and the forest eased to life, bathing the foliage in a soft, warm light. The trio cut their flashlights and the forest murk settled in again.

"I'm fine," Sage replied, her pulse not quite steady. The threat hammered the last remaining nail into her fate.

"We saw a fire. Do I need to do anything?" Ricky asked. With his shaved head, he stood warrior-like, ready to slay her foes. Jessica had assigned the forty-year-old warlock to Sage under duress. Sage's duress. She wasn't ready for the three warlocks a High Priestess required. Ricky was enough. Though not a warlock she ever wanted to sex it up with. Too old, too much in love with another coven witch. The way she wanted it. She didn't want biases disrupting his split duties. And he wielded her witch-fire well. Her bonding familiar, Ice, flitted on his neck, speckled-white feathers against the collar of his black T-shirt.

"No. I doused the fire," she replied, trying to process the freaky situation.

He led the procession to the house, Jessica taking up the tail.

"What happened?" Aspen clutched Sage's arm to her side. "You shouldn't be alone with the circus in town. Why didn't you call Ricky to escort you home?" Tendrils of Aspen's long red hair escaped the ponytail she wore when working in her lab. She already wore a purple work apron, and rosemary and echinacea wafted off the coven's young healer and alchemist.

Sage invoked an air mask over her nose to filter the herbs aggravating her sinuses. "I've walked this path a million times." Sage plodded forward, the aether ache receding into the alcohol-induced implosion of her entire head. The eye grit cleared, but her inner turmoil refused to abate. "I don't know what happened. Some douchebag attacked me, and I defended myself against a few familiars." She knocked her head against Aspen's head. "My aether magic surfaced," she whispered.

Aspen ground to a standstill. "Wait, what?" Sage

pushed at her to move, not wanting Jessica to freak out.

"This incident is why you need another warlock. Rules dictate it, Sage," Jessica admonished. "Too many witches and warlocks are on the property for the festival. It's too risky to wander alone."

Sage tossed up her arms. "Okay. I get it. Sheesh. Can I go take a shower?" She stretched her arms, feeling the ache of fatigue in her bones, as she mentally prepped for the day ahead and the need for peak performance. Now more than ever. The foursome trooped forward, silent, lost in thought.

Aspen fractured the peace for Sage's ears only. "Long time since your aether's popped up. What triggered it?"

Sage gnawed on her bottom lip. "I guess the threat to me." But it was more. Way more. Way too much magic on the property confused her senses.

"You've had plenty of threats without your aether interfering. Your magic bonked you on the head for a reason."

"You think?" Sage grumbled. "Don't tell anyone. Not even Jessica." Ricky led the witches out of the surrounding forest and toward the expansive gardens of the Wilde backyard.

The early morning sun had risen higher in the sky, its light reflecting off the dew-covered grass ahead of them. The myriad green shades of the leaves and evergreens became more vibrant, and the shadows receded toward the forest. Birds chirped their morning song, and Sage left behind the serene forest, as if it hadn't just crapped all over her day.

The path they'd left behind was one of two connecting the backyard to the meadow beyond the woods, where tents had arisen over the last day or two as witches and warlocks converged upon the Wilde property. Not all stayed in tents. Some High Priestesses claimed the spare bedrooms in the mansion, some in the cabins on the property, or booked hotel rooms in nearby Santa Cruz to enjoy peace and harmony along the Pacific coast. Others planned to drive in each day, like the Helwigs who lived in the small town of Scotts Valley, a stone's throw up the highway.

Blooming roses, hydrangeas, and other flowers grew in abundance in rock-faced planters. Home grounded her, and she reveled in the beauty of their gardens. She dipped her hand in the tinkling, three-tiered water fountain in the center of the lawn and created a whirlpool in the largest bowl. Tiny floating water lilies appeared and swirled in the whirlpool. Sage's earth magic at play.

They halted on the sparsely populated patio. Still early for the overnighters to awaken after a day of travel and reunions. The aroma of coffee, eggs, and bacon wafted out of the open doors. Sage would kill for a pot of caffeine.

"Was it a Helwig?" Jessica asked. "Did you ID the familiars?"

"I suspect Zelda." Sage rubbed her aching forehead. "Does she have a bobcat? I need to hear the familiars again to tag them."

"Yep. Bob-kitties," Aspen quipped as she dug through her fanny pack and produced a tiny vial. She uncorked it and handed it to Sage. "Drink up, buttercup."

"Energy or pain?" Sage sucked down the concoction, grimaced, and smacked her lips to rid it of the vile taste.

"Pain. I'll give you a spelled charm for energy

later."

"Thanks." Sage tossed the vial onto a patio table. The glass tube pinged against the tempered glass tabletop and bounced to the pavers, taking Sage's patience with it.

"The Helwigs weren't here yesterday. They're day trippers." Ricky scratched his chin, his fingers following the outline of his goatee. "I'll send a team of warlocks to investigate in full light."

"We'll figure it out later. I need to prep for the day." Sage eyeballed her short skirt and the ash and dirt streaks on her legs. "Thanks for the assist." She elbowed past Ricky through the French doors into the great room. Multicolored Tiffany lamps shed luminous light in the corners of the room, jeweled reflections bouncing off the decorative wall mirrors scattered around her favorite room. Her warlock and aunt beat a hasty retreat. Aspen not so much, as the clack of her sandals followed Sage.

"Walk of shame, sis? How much did you drink? How many warlocks did you boink?"

Sage turned and fixed Aspen with an icy stare. "Big deal. Partying on the first night is a given. I'll adult the rest of the festival." *The rest of my freaking life. Le sigh.*

"Did you really wash it out of your system?" Aspen's light and frothy voice followed Sage up the staircase to their bedrooms. "Who'd you bang?"

On the landing at the top of the stairs, Sage recoiled. "Joshua." She paused. "I don't know his last name. Thought he might contain powerful magic that'd play well with my fire, but he's not all that. Arrived with the Sacramento covens."

"Well, you do need two more warlocks. Them's the rules. What's he all about?"

"He's all about pleasing himself and ensuring any woman he's screwing does nothing but please *him*." Sage gripped the railing overlooking the great room.

"Oh. My. God." Aspen quaked with amusement. "Does he know who you are? Did he want you to bond him?"

"Yes, and hell to the yes. You know I only sleep with the unbonded to test them out. We had fun until we hit the sack. So much lost potential, so little magic."

"Wow. You'd think he'd flip over backward for the opportunity. You picked *him* from all those warlocks vying for your attention last night?" Aspen belly-laughed, pressing on her middle.

"Dial it down, dimwit. You'll wake the house." Sage cupped her hand over her sister's mouth. "Massive error in judgement. I thought he'd at least know what to do with his mega dick. What do you expect from a twenty-one-year-old? Plus, the magic in his aura's half-assed. The sex was so bad I couldn't figure out what element he'd wield."

"So he wagged his mega dick at the wrong sage bush?"

"He's better suited to you, Aspen tree." Sage snorted and trod to her room. "Take him for a spin. At twenty, you'd teach him a thing or three. Maybe he'd get over himself. A big dick's not enough."

"No, thanks. Don't want your sloppy seconds. I've heard all I want to hear about Mr. Ginormous Selfish Prick."

Poor Joshua will never live it down now that Aspen knew. Word among the covens would spread like a wildfire in the drought-stricken forest. The dingleberry drank his weight in tequila and might grovel at her feet later. If he even remembered he'd screwed the highest of the High Priestesses in the region, before he'd fallen asleep on top of her, his mega dick shriveling to a wet noodle inside her. The lame incident forced her to incant air spells to muzzle his snoring and to escape his dead weight.

Solstice festivals typically ended with Sage hammered and in bed with a delectable warlock who wanted Sage to bond him after rejection at the warlock lottery. One last chance for a warlock to snag a witch. Bonding was the only way a warlock could use magic. Without a witch's bond, the warlock sensed an empty core, an impression of a piece missing inside him. A powerful witch sensed the magic in his aura waiting to be tapped. Joshua had a skosh of magic, but not enough for Sage. Her powerful magic would probably kill him.

"What does it say about my dumbass choices?" she bellyached on her way to her parents' former bedroom. Sage closed the double doors to the primary suite, drowning her sister's retreating giggles. She'd taken over the reins from her mother as High Priestess of the Wilde coven and the California region. Today, she'd take over her mother's position to rule the entire West once the Council counted the votes and invested her in the position. The youngest High Priestess ever to rule an entire region. She had uber big shoes to fill.

Sage had put her own stamp on the bedroom to curb her constant grief, and never tired of gazing out the large windows overlooking the backyard and forest beyond. Her sanctuary. Fairy lights hung on the trees surrounding the entire backyard, installed for the festival, and they still glowed on the trees like diamonds on fire. The sun burned away the coastal fog seeping into the mountains, but a fog bank hung over distant Santa Cruz on the Monterey Bay. Lights popped on in the cabins, greeting the dawn of a long day of gatherings and ceremony on the Summer Solstice, the longest day of the year.

The morning crashed into her again. Dread and vulnerability deluged her, and she refused to surrender to their insidious nature. Sage refused to believe someone had the balls to threaten her on her own land. Senses on high alert, she was prepared to take action if another attack came.

No way did she plan to allow the other witch to get one over on her. Magic had lingered in the woods, in the flaming arrow, in the gremlins waving their forks and knives at her. Sage had more than one enemy among the California witches who thought she'd destroy them all because of her youth and because she was a Wilde—and wild—witch. Sage had suffered the pressure since her mother's death and since her aunt Jessica abdicated her position as next in line. She refused to let her coven down. She'd had a year to get her act together. The year had ended, and she didn't plan on losing it all.

"It's *my* birthright. Line in the sand drawn." Sage's skirt shimmied down to her ankles, and she tore her blouse over her head. "They won't see *me* coming. I'll show them all."

Chapter 3

By the time Sage cleaned up, fueled with half a pot of strong coffee and a strawberry and granola yogurt parfait, she was ready. Ten o'clock on the dot. Time to confront her fans in prep for the Council meeting.

"Fans my ass." She pasted on a smile she didn't feel and tucked the front of her dropped-shoulder blouse into her casual summer skirt.

Noise escalated from the great room as she descended the wide, circular staircase. Although she'd taken aspirin and another pain potion Aspen had given her, her headache lingered. Not all of it tequila induced. Sound dropped when she entered the great room, and all eyes landed on her.

Potted plants in every corner carried the outdoors into the room. Bouquets and garlands of summer flowers garnished the room in abundance. Fresh evergreen and roses perfumed the air filtering in through the wide-open windows and patio doors. Her paradise and the perfect cure for her lingering hangover.

"Eat, drink, and be merry. Don't let my presence kill the mood. This is an informal space," she said. Clinks and clatters of silverware on plates resumed, as did the voices of chitchat and laughter. Formal ceremonies occurred in the witch-house or at other designated sites on the grounds, but never in the house. The joint rooms reminded her of family, love, and all the happy times growing up, and she refused to spoil it with business.

Mirrors and landscape paintings decorated the walls between the many windows. Comfortable couches and chairs took up the lion's share of space. Sculpted pillars divided the great room from the dining room, every spot at the twelve-seater table occupied by witches and warlocks. Sage luxuriated in the beauty and comfort of the room before real life snatched control.

Ricky jogged to her from the rock-faced fireplace. He'd already scanned the house for threats or he'd never allow her down the stairs. With the festival going full tilt, too many people were on the grounds for comfort.

"Don't tell anyone what happened this morning," she murmured.

"Only Aspen and Jessica know," he replied. "I've sent out a few feelers, though."

"Good." She shifted toward the French doors flung open to the patio. Long-haired Joshua with his massive dick and abs to die for glowered at her. Anger reddened his cheeks and flushed down his neck.

Who peed in his cup? He has no right to anger. Unless Aspen already circulated smack about him. Oh, hell. Sage cut through the room, closing the distance between them. "Joshua," she greeted. No smile, no touch.

"Why did you leave?" he blurted out. "We were having a blast." He hadn't brushed his long, rocker hair. Threads curled around his well-defined cheekbones and his two-day stubble. Cute, but not for her.

Sage's eyebrows arched. "I wasn't aware I needed your approval."

"But I wasn't done," he sputtered. "I mean, I thought—"

"Done?" She kinked her head to the left. "You pleasured *yourself* and fell asleep on top of me without giving two shits about my pleasure. I guess *you* were done." Snickers rose from the nearby chairs.

He shook his head as if flinging off fleas. "Bull. You spelled me, witch." His frustrated voice echoed through the patio and dining room, leaving a palpable silence in its wake.

Sage decided to teach him a well-needed lesson. Whoever dragged him to the festival hadn't versed him on the rules. Or on who was who.

Aspen ran to Sage for backup and stood by her side. "Hey, *big* guy." Her gaze flickered to the crotch of his board shorts. "Suppose you don't know who you're talking to here, do ya?" She hugged Sage's arm to her side and let go.

"Just another witch." He lifted one shoulder, let it drop. "The one who brought me said she might grant me warlock powers and that I might join a coven. It's why we're here, me and my buds." He swished his toned arm toward two stud muffins on the patio surrounding the table where the Bay Area coven witches sat eating.

"Well, Joshua," Sage said, loud enough for onlookers to hear. The words she meant to say to embarrass him faltered in her mind. Pausing, she pulled her train of thought in a different direction. What would Mom do or say? The crux of the matter. She needed to grow up and fast, or her world promised to crumble into dust and blow into the Pacific.

Sage stuck her hand out to Joshua. "Hello, Joshua. I'm High Priestess Sage Wilde of the Santa Cruz Wilde Coven." The blooming spots of pink on his face deepened. Sage tensed to avoid the vein ready to pop in his jaw. He shook her hand, his palm damp and rough. "You're on my covenstead as my invited guest. I might've said or done something last night or early this morning under the guise of alcohol. If so, I apologize. Now, if you'd like to meet some nice witches who're searching for a warlock to bond, I can introduce you." She paused, and couldn't silence herself from saying for his ears only, "One or two witches who'll teach you the fine arts of pleasing a woman... in bed. You have the tool..."

A sunbeam caught on a mosaic glass candle holder on a patio table and towed her attention beyond Joshua and the steam billowing out of his collar. Sunlight winked off the mosaic and shot across the patio to a pair of young men talking together, one so enticing his appearance stalled her heartbeat for a second. Whatever Joshua said in response and every other sound in the room glided away.

The gorgeous stranger stood next to a warlock, someone she recognized from another coven, but couldn't name him. Neither had vied for her attention last night. Had they just arrived? A sense of intrigue sifted through Sage as she perused the stranger. Tall, dark, and divinely built. Short, layered chestnut hair framed his tan face, his striking chiseled cheekbones, and strong, aquiline nose over full sensuous lips.

Powerful energy emanated from him even from her distance. The unbonded stranger was no ordinary warlock. He possessed intriguing powers. Powers she hungered to uncover.

Aspen nudged Sage's arm, but the words her sister uttered flew in one ear and out the other, not stopping at "go" and collecting two hundred bucks. Dazed, Sage sidestepped past Joshua and strolled onto the patio. Curiosity killing her inner cat, she headed toward the two men.

As she watched The One with every step closer, something about him compelled her. She couldn't stop approaching him even if she wanted to. Powerful, innate, he was more than his gorgeous visage and tall height that made her five-nine height appear short. He had muscles to die for beneath his short-sleeve T-shirt and snug jeans. She needed to know Mr. Freaking Gorgeous ASAP. Both warlocks' gazes settled on her and stuck. Their surprise and fascination twisted into her own awed senses. Had she found her first chosen warlock to bond? The warlock every High Priestess in the western region demanded she bond? Her literal *First Warlock*? The prospects crammed her with a buzzing excitement.

The man standing beside Tall, Dark, and Dreamy bowed his head, prodded the other to do the same. "Greetings, High Priestess Wilde," he said, following formal witchworld rules.

"Hey," The One said, tripping over the word. "Um, High Priestess Wilde."

His voice! Oh, goddess, his smooth baritone set off a fountain between her legs. His gaze never ceased slurping her up, crawling from her ankle boots to the roots of her long, loose blonde hair. Heat assailed her, and she invoked witch-air to fan her face. Her hair wafted in the breeze she created, and she killed the spell to avoid detection.

"Hello—" She started to say "boys," but they were all men. "Gentlemen. Who brought you to the festival?"

"I'm Sammy Luchese. Came with the Scotts Valley coven this morning." He elbowed his friend. "This mute is my bud Rafael Reyes. Came with me, but he's unbonded."

Sage's eyebrows hiked up again. Might be a permanent hike if she didn't watch it. "So you're bonded."

"A Helwig witch bonded me at the Autumn Solstice festival."

The surname of her arch-nemeses couldn't dampen Sage's fascination and the lust raging in her womanly parts. "So, Rafael." She inclined her head at him in acknowledgement. "Can you speak?" A smile teased the corners of her lips.

He cleared his throat, scratched his jaw. "Sorry. Yeah." Golden glimmers twinkled in his awestruck whiskey-colored eyes.

With a sudden sharpness, Sage realized she needed him more than anything else in her life. More than air. "Have you pledged to a witch yet?"

"Not sure what that means." He slid a questioning glance at Sammy.

"He's lost." Sammy grinned, displaying impeccable white teeth, no doubt a victim of teen braces. Red streaks in his short, choppy auburn hair glittered under the rising sun. Though Sammy was a few inches shorter than Rafael, his toned and powerful body would make any witch feel safe entrusting him with her magic. The typical warlock, hence the reason they made perfect guards. "Thought

I'd help him find someone who'd give him the four-one-one."

Rafael's innate tug on her fire intrigued the hell out of her. As if he'd reached into her aether core and snapped handcuffs on her magic, and only he held the key. As though he possessed his own magic that harmonized with hers. The residual aether glowed bright and warm inside Sage, but the good side of the aether coin. She wanted to bathe in it and melt under his hands, his lips, under his entire body. Why hadn't *he* attended the party last night instead of Joshua?

"Well, Sage Wilde," a hateful, grating voice infringed upon the moment. "I see you've met my recruit." The witch glided to a standstill beside Rafael, not bothering to give Sage the proper greeting of one in a higher station. Ire turned her stomach into a tight ball. Zelda's rosewater perfume overwhelmed the air. Not a scent she'd smelled in the woods earlier. Not that it mattered. Could've been any Helwig minion following orders.

Sage rotated her body a bit toward the older witch. Older by at least thirty years. Not unattractive unless you counted her uppity, snarky attitude, evilness, and spitefulness. No pointy hat or pointy-toed boots graced her all-black attire and board-straight black hair.

"Well met, Zelda." Sage nodded at the Helwig witch. "Did you just arrive?" Or did you attack me in the woods earlier? Sage's unspoken question begged for an answer.

"Yes. My sister and I are excited for the Council meeting today." She linked her arm in Rafael's and his startled gaze bounced from Sage to Zelda. "Now, my dear boy, it's time we got better acquainted." Sammy bowed to Sage, and Zelda guided the two men toward the woods.

A twinge of jealousy ripped through Sage's fury. As she watched Rafael disappear down the flagstones, she couldn't shake the feeling that her path promised to cross his again. Anticipation fluttered in her chest, diminishing her anger. She made a mental note to find ways in her busy schedule to seek him out. Rafael Reyes in the mix guaranteed an exciting adventure and a hopeful future. Despite Zelda laying her claim and the rules of poaching a witch's warlock. Warlocks retained a choice, and she'd damn well ensure Rafael chose correctly.

Chapter 4

Disoriented, Rafael walked away from the alluring blonde witch, the smell of her perfume still enticing him. The intensity of her gaze lingered on him. Lust barreled through him, and he wanted to zip back to her, touch her, and feast his sight on her. Her curves shot his desire into overdrive, and he itched to touch her, to ensure she wasn't an illusion. Was the weird internal connection he felt real?

As he walked into the woods toward the Helwigs' designated spot on the fringes of the meadow, that connection wrenched on him. Tried to lure him back. To the most beautiful and bewitching woman he'd ever seen. Her long, wavy hair glinted like spun gold in the morning sunlight. She was so damn hot. The sight of Sage Wilde's captivating beauty made his heart skip a beat, like fate had delivered. As if the universe had chosen him to experience something special in coming to the festival.

He'd accompanied Sammy not just for a good time,

although God knows he needed to party, but Sammy also said he might learn about himself. It wasn't until they'd arrived at the Helwigs' property that Sammy divulged what he meant. Until that morning, he had no clue Sammy was a warlock and derived magic from a witch. The witchworld had remained in total darkness in Rafael's mind, until Sammy hinted Rafael was probably a warlock. Which explained nothing. Which explained a shit-ton about why he didn't know his family roots or what was living inside him. Until he met Sage Wilde, and that thing inside him stirred like never before. About to scurry back to her, he halted and Zelda's arm fell from his.

"Something wrong?" the witch asked. Sammy came up short behind him and nearly brained himself against Rafael's back.

"Sorry, man." Rafael stumbled on his words, so tongue-tied from the revelations opening up his mind. "That girl, Sage, who is she?"

Zelda's perpetual frown shifted to a deadpan look of hatred. "*Girl* is about right. You don't need to distract yourself with Sage Wilde. She's too busy screwing everything on two legs and drinking herself under the table."

"Wait, I thought she's the High Priestess of the entire California region." Sammy shuffled his sneakers in the pea gravel lining the path. "Aren't the coven heads supposed to vote her in as the western region High Priestess? Pretty damn young for such a prime position."

An epic scowl altered Zelda's half-assed pretty face to an old hag. Rafael almost slunk into the woods to avoid catching whatever crawled up her ass.

"Yes, well, we'll see how over-stacked the deck is today," Zelda spat out, mega distaste and jealousy in her words. "Witchworld laws and rules have a mind of their own, and the goddess always seems to favor the Wildes. They've been a thorn in the Helwigs' sides for eons." She linked her arms again with Rafael and Sammy, inserting herself between them. Her clinch so tight, Rafael felt like a purchased man with no will of his own. He had no choice but to tag along. After all, she was his plus-two with Sammy. A plus-one? Who knew? But she wasn't the witch he wanted touching him. Not by a long shot.

"Come, gentlemen. I want to test Rafael's powers. I believe I may want to bond you myself." She practically drooled on Rafael's arm. "You're too valuable for a lesser witch. That blonde twit doesn't have my experience, or the two elemental powers I possess. She's not ready for a warlock of your potential."

Ants crawled up his spine. *Did* he have a choice? Or was he trapped? Crazy visuals he could do without. "I don't understand. How do you know I'm a warlock?" He yanked his arm out of her ironclad clasp and pinned both arms to his sides. He needed her not touching him.

She released Sammy. "Sweet boy, most warlocks don't know they contain magic until a witch opens the doors. Sammy, tell him how Helena found you."

"Dude." Sammy guided him to a cement garden bench in the woods.

Trees stretched toward the sky in the woods surrounding the bench. Leaves and evergreen boughs rustled in the breeze, casting dappled shadows on the forest floor, creating shadows on his thoughts. The sweet perfume of summer pines permeated the air, not enough to overpower Zelda's cloying rose perfume. The rough texture of the cement bench under him and the solid earth beneath his feet grounded him. He appreciated the beauty of the woods, but he couldn't ignore the subtle undercurrent of danger around him.

"Take a chill pill. These witches know their stuff, man. You hold magic in your aura and they sense it. Your real magic will come from the witch who bonds you." Sammy flung out his hand, tossing an invisible band of air around Rafael, binding him to the bench. Rafael struggled against another ironclad hold, fuming, fire roasting his face.

"Helena's an air witch," Zelda added. "She found Sammy ready to toss himself off a cliff into the bay last year. The untapped magic inside him languished too long before being tapped. The poor boy couldn't handle the disorder and depression, not knowing why he felt he didn't fit within the human world."

Sammy grinned and released his band, the air whooshing from around Rafael, ruffling the sleeves of his T-shirt. He shook himself like a dog flinging off water and leaped onto the bench, and then into the air. A pillow of air cushioned his landing on a crumbling tree stump.

"Dude, the moment Helena bonded me, I found myself." Sammy slapped Rafael on the back. "She's taught me a crap-ton about the witchworld and magic. She's not a bad lay either."

"Wait, what?" Rafael wagged his head, sending his hair flying around his temples. "You've been seeing Melissa for two years. You cheated on her?"

"No, man." Sammy gave Rafael the hand. "Sex with a witch is a way for her to gauge abilities since mine weren't obvious. Also strengthens the bond."

"It's time you cut ties to Melissa, Sammy." Zelda linked her arm in his again, sending another crawl of ants down Rafael's spine. "Melissa doesn't fit in our world. If you can't break it off, Helena can gently turn her against you."

Zelda's words registered, and the ants dug holes in Rafael's skin. He held his tongue, waited for Sammy to blast the bitch a new one.

"Yes, Ms. Helwig. I understand," Sammy responded, his reluctance evident in the drooping of his shoulders.

Shock suffused Rafael, and he jerked off the bench to his feet. "Do you hear yourself, man?"

"Sammy. Return to our campsite." Without another word, Sammy strode off, flinging a last pleading glance over his shoulder at Rafael.

"Rafael, my dear." Zelda gripped his wrist, her fingernails digging into his skin, forcing him to follow her into the woods behind a giant redwood. She rose on her toes and dropped a kiss on his mouth, her sweet berry lipstick shooting heat to his groin. He was powerless to kill the lust barreling through him. Had she spelled him?

"It's best this way. Non-magicals cause problems, and using magic around them could unintentionally hurt them. Do you want Sammy to harm Melissa by accident?" He shook his head. "This is a price to join the witchworld. In return, you receive powers you've never dreamed of. You'll belong to people who'll embrace you and *never* let you down." Zelda squeezed his biceps and rubbed her thin body against him, doubling her efforts at his crotch. An instant erection caused her full-throated laughter. "And you can have all the sex you want. The Helwig witches share our warlocks well. Plus, with the power I sense in you, you can become a warlock leader." She squeezed her fingers inside the waistband of his jeans and raked her long fingernails down his hard length. "Doesn't that sound divine?"

Emitting a groan, he unbuttoned his jeans to relieve the pressure, and Zelda slid his zipper down. The zipper's rasp incited his lust further. Nodding, Rafael pressed his erection into her hand now going to town on him. The shrill screech of a blue jay over his head whacked sense into him. People talking on the pathway forced him to jerk her hand out of his pants.

Horror swamped him, an instant buzzkill. "Stop," he rasped out. His head spun, and he darted into the woods. He jogged as fast as the terrain allowed until he confronted the edge above a shallow ravine, panting against a boulder cropping out of the earth, signaling the descent. Readjusting his pants, he flinched when his jeans pressed on his now deflating erection.

Closing his eyes, he leaned a hip on the boulder until his breathing leveled out. *What the hell was that crazy business?* He felt no attraction to the witch! After a year-long dry spell, he was long overdue, but it wasn't the witch's hand his mind's eye felt. All he pictured was Sage Wilde stroking him.

"What the fuck?" He slid down to the ground, nudging aside a rock poking into his butt. He scrubbed his face and stretched out his legs. No telling how long he sat, soaking in the sun filtering through the sparser trees when he heard a rustling in the nearby brush. His eyes shot open.

"Rafael? Are you okay?"

Sage Wilde, goddess personified. The sun shimmered off her hair, haloing her in gold. He rubbed his eyelids and blinked a few times, sure he was dreaming and expecting the scene to fade.

"Rafael?"

He lurched up off the ground, steadying his hip

against the boulder. She tossed her hair over her shoulder, holding her head high. A confidence in her stride ratcheted up her attraction tenfold. "Sage, I mean, High Priestess—"

She held up a hand and gave him the most radiant smile he'd ever seen. Her pink-frosted lips spread, revealing a straight line of perfect white teeth. The sun sparkled in her green eyes, disbursing grass-green flecks among the emeralds.

"No need for formalities at our festivals. You're a witchworld guest."

"Not what that Helwig witch said."

"Yeah, well, *that Helwig witch* is a witch." She giggled, and he about melted in the tinkling, cheerful sound. "You're on my covenstead. I make the rules."

"You're pretty young to rule." He craved to know her, but he didn't know if he'd just insulted her or handed her props.

She laughed, not at all insulted, and his heart beat again. "Yep. Happens when your parents careen off a cliff in the Tahoe Mountains. I'm the oldest of the three daughters they left behind, so it's my turn to rule." Pain deadened the radiance in her eyes. "It's my time to adult."

"I'm sorry." Before he thought better of it, he touched his right fingers to her forearm. She caught his hand in her own. Fire erupted between them, roaring up his arm and down his chest, triggering his heart to thunder anew. That unnamed thing—no other defined name existed—deep in his core connected to the fire and zoomed through his body.

Sage's eyes rounded, and instead of releasing his hand to extinguish the flames from broiling them alive, she linked her fingers in his. A blustery wind fanned her silky hair over her shoulders. Water misted them both from a clear blue sky, only somewhat cooling his jets. Her fire burned unabated inside him, and he wanted it, needed it. He didn't know if he'd survive another minute without her. Rafael gripped her hand so tight she yelped.

"Sorry." Without releasing her, he relaxed his hold.

She beamed her luminous smile. "No prob. I like your strength." She drew him closer, close enough to kiss. "Why are you by the ravine?"

Dropping her hand, he dug his hands into his front pockets and hunched over. "Needed to clear the storm out of my head."

She jolted backward. "Really? This is the path I take to declutter my head when too many people hound me. No one comes out this far."

"Like minds." Witch protocols swirled in his head. "I thought you always had a warlock guard."

"I *have* a warlock here." She winked, and a part of him dissolved.

The way she said the words, honest and intimate, set him on fire again. Lust speared to his dick. Instant tent pitch. He'd never gotten aroused from a woman's mere voice. Had she also plunked a spell on him? What's with these witches?

Her head dipped, and he realized he hadn't zipped up his jeans. The evidence of his arousal bulged out between them. *Dumbass.*

Eyes twinkling, she said teasingly, "Umm, did I interrupt a date... with your hand?"

His laughter boomed, and he felt the heat of his embarrassment fading. "That Helwig witch couldn't keep *her* hands off me." He released Sage's hand to zip up his pants, and she tried to stop him.

"Not on my account." Her teasing, lilting voice

turned his erection to steel.

Were these witches for real? He was smack-dab stuck in one of those sappy romance novels his last foster mom read, like a love triangle. Without the love. He'd arrived in an alternate reality, and he feared never finding himself again. A frigid revulsion iced the heat swamping him, and he backed away from her, held up his hands to stop her from closing the gap.

"Stay away from me," he ordered.

Sage's face sagged, and she hugged her arms over her chest. "What did I do?"

"You witches are trouble. I see it now. I don't belong here." But he did belong, not just because he desired Sage; he still tasted the sweetness of her coconut and vanilla perfume on his tongue. Magic hummed in every fiber of his being. Her magic. Confusion stirred the tempest in his head, pain battering his skull. He needed time to digest, away from Sage and this covenstead.

"Rafael, my magic mingled with *yours*. You *do* belong."

"Nope. I don't have magic. I'm just a normal guy." He backed up another step as if the extra space promised to temper the simmering pot in his core.

"Oh. Okay." Sage seemed to accept his words, but her disappointment gutted him. Uncertainty gutted him. "I believe you're a warlock," she continued. "It's why we connected"—she gestured at his middle—"so easy."

"I didn't connect to Helwig. She told me my magic wouldn't manifest until a witch bonded me," he spat the words out.

"True for most witches and warlocks. You're powerful, and I don't need to bond you to sense your magic. There's magic inside you. You have a powerful aura, which connects to my magic. But I, or another witch, need to bond you for you to use the magic. I can explain more later."

"Not buying it." But the fizzing airy fire inside him negated his words. His frustration tripped off the rails. He didn't know right from left, and searched for a hole in the ground to sink into. The tree-studded ravine looked like a perfect haven.

Sage forced a thin, tight-lipped smile. "Do you want to leave the festival?"

Hell to the yes. No fucking way. "Yes." The only word he managed to croak out, whether right or wrong.

Chapter 5

I n a tense silence, Sage trudged toward the backyard gardens, and Rafael followed at a lengthening distance. He puzzled her. Her magic connected to his powerful aura, when she should've only sensed his potent magic. She'd never met such a powerful warlock before bonding, not that she'd bonded many. Ricky was the only warlock currently bonded to her. The crux of her situation. Council rules dictated a High Priestess must have three warlocks for protection. Since she was close to becoming the regional leader, she had to bury her procrastination and fill her dance card. Bonded to a powerful warlock like Rafael might allow her to escape the three-warlock rule for a while. She'd have to bond him to find out for real. No need for sex, despite her intense desire to dance that waltz. Holy hell, she wanted him even if he wasn't a warlock.

Lost in her random thoughts, she tripped on an old fallen branch. She yelped as she tipped forward, angling toward the ground. Before taking a header,

Rafael caught her from behind, his arms encircling her waist. She liquified against his sinfully hard body, loving the feel of his muscular arms around her.

She clamped on to his arm across her middle. "I'm such a klutz. Thanks for the save. Bruises and broken bones might ruin my rep at the Council meeting."

"Do you mean the rep of a doesn't-give-a-fuck party girl?" His mouth hovered near her left ear, and a shiver worked its way across her shoulders.

She cringed. "You heard the stories?"

"Only what Zelda Helwig spewed." His arm eased upward until it lodged beneath her breasts. "Is it true?"

She trailed her bare fingernails over his arm, loving the steel beneath his warm skin. "I'm young. I socialize." Rafael exuded a tantalizing scent of spice and citrus, like a forbidden temptation.

"Do you screw every warlock you meet?" His stomach sucked in.

White-hot rage bristled through Sage. She peeled both his arms off her torso.

Shame mottling his skin, he hung his head. "Sorry. Not my business. I'll hit it now."

"No," Sage demanded in her High Priestess voice, meant for all in her world to obey. Rafael dropped his arms and stood stock-still, his dark whiskey eyes somber. "The witchworld grants High Priestesses leniencies, and it includes screwing any unattached or unbonded warlock we want. Having sex with a warlock can strengthen the bond between them. I can recite the bonding spell when we are both at our most vulnerable. We also use the act to test a warlock's strength. A witch can't grant a warlock her magic until she establishes a bond. I also test warlocks for my coven, not just for me."

"So you're a sex goddess?" He snorted.

Sage headed down the path again. Why this man? Why this day? "Yes, Rafael Reyes. I have a lot of sex. Do I enjoy the sex?" The morning's antics and the aftermath vaulted to her mind. "Sometimes. Do I fall in love with a candidate warlock? Nope. Do I bring them to my bed. Hell to the no. Do I do PDA and go on dates? Again, no way. I do my job for my coven. I do it because I'm the most powerful Wilde witch alive. I can determine what magic a warlock would excel at by touching him. Sometimes it takes more than a touch. I'm a matchmaker between my witches and warlocks. And if I find a warlock who doesn't fit in our coven, I send him to another coven where I believe he might fit. But he has a choice. He can leave the witchworld and never look back. Or he can leave and return anytime he wants. Our world is centuries old. This is our way." Perspiration dripped between her breasts.

The sound of their shoes on the pebble pathway and the approaching music and people playing games pervaded the air, but didn't make a dent in the moment's seriousness. The festivity had driven the birds and small forest animals deeper into the woods, the place where Sage wanted to run to escape the rest of her life. She missed the white noise of the birds teasing her owl familiars.

Sage hit the split in the path and stepped onto the right fork leading to the house. Without changing direction, she slowed her roll. "See ya, Rafael. You're welcome to stay. Check the schedule posted by the witch-house, the barn-like structure. Festival ends tomorrow at five." She didn't wait for a response and was almost running by the time she reached the rear patio.

Wishing he'd followed her, she checked over her

shoulder, but he'd vanished. Wherever he went, he lugged along a tiny piece of her heart. Something so fundamental hurt inside her. Her aether stirred restlessly, more than it had earlier. Everything inside her begged her to seek him out and continue their conversation. To convince him to stay. To encourage him to accept her, the sole warlock she'd ever wanted to bond. Not only bond, but to allow him in *her* bed. Her bedroom, her sanctuary.

Aspen skipped down the path, two frozen tropical drinks in her hands, rainbow cocktail umbrellas fluttering in the breeze. She extended one to Sage. "You look like you need a daiquiri."

Just the look of the fruity concoction in the glass soured her stomach. "No, thanks. I've had my fill for the week. Hell, the entire month."

Aspen's eyelashes flapped, her mouth transforming into a flycatcher. "What? Sage Wilde is rejecting a shindig in a glass." She rested a frosty glass against Sage's forehead. "Do you need a happy pill?" She rotated to the side and dropped her arm. "Back pocket. Energy potion."

Sage grabbed both glasses and set them on a nearby table, tempted to dump them out. "It's not even noon. And you're underage."

Aspen snatched one drink and stuck the straw in her mouth, took two deep draws. "It's noon somewhere. And I'm almost twenty-one."

Sage frowned, hoping and searching the yard for Rafael. "You seen Ricky?"

Aspen dug a vial out of her pocket and handed it to Sage. "He's pissed you took off."

Sage accepted the tiny vial and sucked down the contents. She needed witch-style energy to slide through the day. Gagging, she stammered, "Jeez, are you off your meds? Is this poison?"

Aspen grinned. "New potion I'm working on. Flavor comes later. I'm meeting the other alchemists tomorrow to trade notes."

"Good. You need to bounce ideas. Mom taught you well of the old potions, charms, and spells, but she didn't add to her arsenal often. It's time for you to jazz things up."

"Exactly. I got gummies, mints, and other ideas floating in the noggin."

Sage's phone beeped with a text. "Ricky spied me. I gotta bounce."

Aspen wasted no time in snagging the other daiquiri and darting down the path. At least Sage didn't have to parent her seventeen-year-old youngest sister, Willow, during the festival. Since Willow hadn't come into her magic yet, she didn't want to attend anything witch related, especially with warlocks hulking around. Willow enjoyed no fond memories of warlocks except their father, a warlock who didn't follow the tradition of witches dominating them, and was their mother's equal. Different from the old witchworld rules. Too modern, too progressive. Sage preferred witches to rule and dominate their warlocks in the way of the old traditions, which included sleeping with any unbonded warlock she chose.

The only warlock she wanted touching her was the fleeing Rafael Reyes. *Why can't I boot him out of my freaking head?*

Burying her thoughts of the mysterious warlock, she scurried to the witch-house. Already, the energy potion warmed her gut, and she felt an extra pep in her step, as her father used to say. Aspen was on to something. Adrenaline rushed through her veins and drove out the dregs of her hangover headache. Was it the potion? Or the idea of bonding Rafael Reyes? A man who didn't know his true identity and wanted no part of the witchworld, the place he clearly—at least to her—belonged. She snickered, not letting those thoughts turn Debbie Downer on her.

The California covens and their individual councils already filled the converted barn. Sage stepped through the open sliding barn doors. They'd arranged long tables in a square. Beverages, lunch, and a myriad of other snacks loaded down tables against the walls. More flowers and vines adorned the witch-house. A pair of witches waved feathers to disburse smoke rising from thick sage sticks to purify the witch-house and prepare for their solstice blessing. Calming lavender bubbled in bowls scattered around the barn to diffuse the sage and any potential tension that might arise.

Jessica motioned for Sage to join her at the head table, though they had another fifteen minutes until the meeting commenced. The Wilde Council included Aunt Jessica, her younger and absent world-traveler, aunt Juliette, Aspen, and Jessica's daughters, twins Marina and Brianne, and the eldest Eden. Bonded warlocks surrounded the perimeter of the room and guarded the two entrances.

Glowering, Ricky joined Sage, the heat of his annoyance leeching down her side. "Don't go off alone without a trusted warlock. Not after this morning."

"I needed to clear my head," she defended.

He growled. "Don't do it again. Not until we get a handle on the sitch."

"What did you find out?" Sage asked.

"Like you said, the arrows were real, not magical. I also found cat scat in the area."

"Zelda's familiar." Jessica scanned the crowd for

the other witch.

"Bitch," Sage blasted out. "It's always the Helwigs fighting for everything the Wildes have earned."

"Wait." Jessica gripped Sage's arm. "You said multiple animals."

Her arm may fall off if one more person locked on to it. Sage licked her bottom lip, thinking. "At least four. Bobcats roam our woods too. But with all the people here, you'd think they'd all scampered for the deep hills."

"Zelda doesn't have four familiars. She has three bonded warlocks, her summoning familiar and her main familiar."

"Her warlocks might've been there," Ricky shot back.

"They would've made too much noise. The Helwigs didn't arrive until just before breakfast." Sage glided her fingernails over her cheek, gnawed on a cuticle.

"Not if they used a protective ward." Jessica released Sage's arm. "My bet's on Zelda."

"We've got her dead to rights," Ricky insisted.

"Hardly." Sage rubbed her arm, trawling a fingernail across her skin. "Still not convinced." She focused on the room at large. "I need to call the meeting to order. Ricky, look and listen for expressions, signs, anything from anyone who's not a friend to the Wildes, or me."

"Already on it."

She fought the desire to fly off—broomstick not required—and escape her duties. She craved Rafael Reyes like no man or warlock she'd ever met. But she needed to suffer through the necessary evils of the Council meeting and festival. Not simply as host, but as the California, and soon the entire western region, High Priestess. Not for the first time did she selfishly wish her mother had never died and held the reins in her rightful place. As the youngest High Priestess in the U.S., Sage hated the weight of the expectations bogging down her shoulders.

Sage clenched the wooden gavel in her right hand and banged it down on the podium three times. The warmth of the smooth, worn wood brought her closer to her mother and grandmother, prior Wilde High Priestesses. The gavel clattered to the podium surface, and the raucous noise in the room dropped to a dull roar until all the witches took their assigned seats. Warlocks stood or sat in chairs behind their witches. Wilde warlocks and witches guarded the doors from the festivalgoers who wandered in by accident.

"Bright blessings and merry met." Sage projected for all to hear. The witches threw out jovial greetings. After the noise died again, she picked up the electronic tablet and read the Midsummer blessing aloud:

Blessed be the turning of the wheel as the sun reaches its zenith on this Summer Solstice. May the warmth and light of this longest day fill us with joy and vitality, and may we be blessed with abundance throughout the season.

May the power of the sun infuse us with courage, strength, and inspiration to pursue our dreams and goals. May we honor the earth and all its creatures, and work to protect and preserve the beauty and balance of the natural world.

As we celebrate the solstice, may we remember the connection of all things

*and the cycles of life and death, growth
and decay. May we embrace change with
open hearts and minds, and may we find
wisdom and guidance in the traditions of
our ancestors.*

*Blessed be the Summer Solstice, and all
the magic it brings.*

Sage banged the gavel down and brought the summer Council meeting to order. Jessica, as the Council secretary, replaced her, and Sage returned to her seat at the head of the table behind the podium.

"First task on our agenda is to announce the vote count to install the western region High Priestess, a position left open when Jana Wilde passed." Grumbles rose from the Helwigs and their allies seated near them, while most of the room projected healthy and positive vibes. "An unbiased third-party counted the vote because of accusations the Wildes might tamper with the election." Jessica's head swiveled to the Helwigs, held a few seconds, and turned back to face the center of the room. "Everyone agreed on the method and agreed to accept the vote as final."

Imelda Helwig, Zelda's younger sister, waved her hand as if swatting a fly. "Get on with it," she mumbled loud enough for everyone to hear.

It wasn't a given that Sage had won. She was young, hence the reason for the vote. If she had been forty-something with ten or twenty years of experience under her pointy hat, no one would've thought twice. Well, no one but their longtime adversaries. Zelda had been hell-bent on merging the small Scotts Valley and Santa Cruz covens for decades. Every attempt at usurping control got thrown in Zelda's face, and she hadn't attempted a coup since Sage's mother became High Priestess. She was shocked Zelda hadn't tried a takeover this year. Maybe the Helwigs had another evil coup up their sleeves. Or maybe Zelda had rigged the vote.

A witch from the unbiased Far Northern California coven handed the locked steel box to Jessica. Ben, Jessica's sole warlock and husband, closed in on her. The voting company had mailed the box to the Far Northern coven and a key to three random-drawn covens. Such was the way of the current witchworld. Dreading the results, no matter which way they swung, Sage pushed out a sigh.

Jessica set the box on the head table. "Does anyone want to inspect the box to ensure no tampering?" She baited the Helwigs, and Sage gave her a mental high five.

Zelda elbowed her sister. "Yes."

Imelda hoofed it to the table, her all-black outfit mimicking her older sister's austere clothing. She wore a large antique moonstone pendant, a permanent fixture around her neck. Sage had never seen her without. The pendant matched a moonstone ring Zelda wore on her left hand, signifying her marriage to her coven. Strands of silver shot through Imelda's lustrous long, black hair. She inspected every side of the box and gave Zelda a thumbs-up. "The Helwig clan has no issues with the vote container. Who received the keys?" The witch scanned one corner of the room to the others.

The Los Angeles and the San Francisco Bay Area High Priestesses stood, and Zelda joined them. Imelda smirked and returned to her seat.

Sage rolled her eyes. Sometimes, she wished she could slither out of these Council meetings and hide under a rock until everyone hit the road. The idea of a magical broomstick sounded awesome. *As if.*

The three witches opened the box and inspected the sealed envelope inside. With deliberate motions, Ben used his pocketknife to slice it open and slipped out the printed vote results. He handed it to Jessica, and the trio of witches lunged for it.

Magic climbed in the air, perceptible to Sage, who had an uncanny knack for sensing magic that escaped other witches. She sprang up, her metal chair folding in on itself and clattering to the wood flooring. "Stop!" Her glare primed to blast a hole in Zelda's forehead. *One could only wish.* "Zelda. Drop the freaking magic. You know magic's not allowed in here."

A bright red flush stole over Zelda's face, her indignation palpable. "You're insane, girl. You're sensing all the witches in the room. Too much for you to handle, huh?"

"Nope. You turned up the knob. Now hit the kill switch." She snatched the gavel and pounded it on the table, the sound reverberating up to the high-beamed ceiling. "Did you spell the letter, trying to destroy it before Jessica reads it? Did you glamour it? Afraid I'm gonna win? You know my name's written all over the results. No one wants you ruling." She'd stepped over the line articulating the thoughts of three-quarters of the room. The witch hag had pushed Sage's last button. Knowing that Zelda wanted Rafael shot her patience to the moon. *All's fair in love and war. Whoa! Where'd the word* love *stem from?*

Warlocks edged closer to their witches. Magic in all the elements flared up in the room as witches prepped their defensive magic. The pungent odor of fertile loam and brimstone overpowered the ineffectual lavender drifting through the air.

Jessica tapped the mic several times, the loud booming and resulting electronic screech quelling a near insurrection. "Shut down the magic and return to your seats. Or we call this meeting off."

"Then what? Sage rules because she's a Wilde?" Zelda sneered.

"Read the vote." Sage stamped her boot on the wooden floor, vibrating several planks. "If you don't agree with the results, tough shit. I'm shitting in the same woods, and you don't see me threatening anyone."

The witches returned to their seats, tense and grumbling. Warlocks stood stalwart and nervous at their prior positions. Residual witch-air billowed through Sage's own witch-air, scattering it. Invisible witch-fire converted the space into an inferno and sweat formed beneath her breasts. A pungent earthy aroma permeated the room, and Sage expected weeds to pop out of the woodwork if she blinked. Remaining vigilant, she opened her senses to detect another magic outburst.

Jessica's hands trembled as she unfurled the paper with the results. "By order of the Western Witch's Council, Sage Wilde is hereby voted in as western regional High Priestess by a majority vote, until she forfeits, loses her magic permanently, is permanently incapacitated, passes to the other side, or receives a *unanimous* regional vote to remove her from office." Jessica handed the paper to the High Priestess on her left. "It is written, so mote it be pursuant to the Book of Shadows, modern edition number three."

The room erupted, a chaotic combination of applause, cheers, and loud dissent from the Helwigs and their minions. Once again, magic seeped into the air, creating a visible mushroom cloud of doom at ceiling height.

Zelda rushed forward, rammed Ben out of the way, and clutched the mic. "You will all rue this day. This chit will never meet your expectations. The government will crack down on all witches and enact laws to hamper our every move. Sage Wilde will destroy the witchworld." The room fell silent to her angry bellows. "I demand a new vote in three months' time, per the rules."

Misty, the Bay Area High Priestess, and a staunch Wilde ally addressed the crowd. "Sage won the vote fair and square. They outvoted you, Zelda. Take it like a lady. Three-quarters of the region don't want a Helwig leader. We all know the history of the Helwigs who dragged us into the Witches and Warlocks war, on the warlock's side, I might add. So zip it and pop a squat."

Sage perched a hip on the table, grim and stone-faced. She'd expected Zelda to screech out a tangent. Fire roiled in her chest, and she wanted to blast the Wicked Witch of the West to smithereens.

Jessica grabbed the mic from Zelda's hand, wincing from the heat Zelda projected on the handle. "If you force another vote, you'll challenge me on the ticket."

Sage gasped and gained her feet. She cupped her hand over the mic. "Aunt Jessica," she whispered. "You abdicated. You said you don't have it in you to rule, and you wanted young blood to carry on our traditions for a longer time."

"Let me finish," Jessica murmured. Sage removed her hand from the mic, and Jessica continued, "Although young, Sage has the smarts, the power, the business and finance degrees to run this region for a good long time. She's the most powerful witch we've seen in decades, if not longer. By the witch's decree, the role is my rightful place in Jana's stead. You'll waste time and money forcing another vote."

Rebel, High Priestess of the Silicon Valley coven and Wilde ally, stood next to Misty. "The vote stands. Sage is our regional High Priestess." Every other witch repeated the words until Sage heard her name chanted over and over. Several of Zelda's best bitches even chanted Sage's name.

The Helwigs' biggest hater from a Southern California coven, whom Sage had a difficult time naming, shouted, "Accept the role, Sage. We need your young blood to carry us into our next chapter. You were born for this. Your mother prepared you for this. No one can take it from you, least not Zelda or Imelda Helwig."

The outpouring of encouragement and acknowledgment stunned Sage. She scrambled up on the table and shouted, "I accept!" Hating the role with everything in her, but wanting to please her deceased parents from the grave, she blew out the candle she'd picked up and accepted her inheritance. "So mote it be."

Chapter 6

Smoke spiraled up from embers raining down upon Sage, and a gust of wind disbursed the fire magic. Zelda released her bobcat familiar, and it dashed toward Sage, stopping short of leaping on the table, teeth bared and tail swishing.

Sage yelped and her pulse quickened. The candle dropped from her hand and clunked onto the floor. Arrows shot from her eyes at Zelda. The bobcat emitted a high-pitched scream, like a hysterical woman, mimicking Zelda. Silence fell upon the room, and Ricky helped Sage clamber off the table. Her temper flared, overpowering her fear. Aether ascended inside her, and her vision grew blurry as agony gathered behind her eyes.

"How dare you threaten me?" Sage didn't miss a beat. "As regional High Priestess, I banish the entire Helwig coven from the solstice event. Now retrieve your familiar before I unleash my ninja fairies on it." Her aether ebbed and flowed, said ninjas raring to go medieval. Sage felt the telltale silver circling her darkening irises. Mirror unnecessary. She ducked her head to hide her shifting eyes from the crowd. "Get me out," she whispered to Ricky. "Now, please."

The wildcat hissed at Sage before Zelda summoned it. It scuttled up her arm, morphing into tattoo form.

Ricky escorted Sage out the rear door. Uncertainty set up a padded room in Sage's mind. The bobcat sounds didn't mirror the animals from her forest escapade. *What the what?*

"What's wrong?" Ricky shut the door behind them. Music and the cheerful clamor of the festival gatherings and games drowned out the racket in the witch-house. Sage tipped her head back for his view, and he recoiled, his shoulders shuddering. "Your aether?" Only a few people in her life had ever seen her aether rising, or even knew about it.

She nodded. "I didn't want anyone to see. For all they know, the bobcat scared me and I left to regroup." She knuckled her eyes, leaned against his bracing arm. "The animals that threatened me this morning sounded different."

"Are you sure?" Ricky led her to a weathered picnic table behind the witch-house, an area off bounds from the festival. He unfolded a dusty lawn chair, and she sagged into it, elbows on her knees, chin in her hands.

"Positive. But she could've used magic to throw me off." The aether retreated into her core, boiling and popping, waiting for Sage's call to action.

"True." Ricky crouched, picking at weeds growing between the pavers. "By the way, congrats."

"Gee, thanks. How does it feel to be the number one warlock of the entire western region?" Ice, her bonding familiar, peeked out from the neck of his T-shirt and cooed at her with adoring eyes.

He grinned, his mouth stretching out his trim goatee. "Can't say I feel any different. Guess I will once you bond three other warlocks, considering I'm only temporary."

Sage waggled her head. "What do you mean temporary?"

Ricky rose and paced the patio. He kicked at more weeds in the pavers, toed pine cones in a pile. Always ready to clean up any mess when Sage needed him. "I want to ask Leah to marry me. I can't be bonded to two witches, and it's not fair to her if I remain tied to you."

"Oh, Ricky. Of course you two must marry and bond." Sage sat back, her eyes normal and her headache a dull throb. "I love Leah. She's a great earth witch to have in my coven and to mentor my cousin." Although not a blood relative, Leah had joined the Wilde coven two years ago. In her mid-thirties and an only child, her parents had moved to Spain and abandoned her except for the occasional phone call. She'd found a home with the Wildes and lived in a cabin on the property with Ricky. "You ready to learn earth magic?" She tossed him a smile.

"How hard can it be? I'll miss your witch-fire though." He held out his hand. "Come on. You need a drink."

"I'll grant you earth magic and you can take it for a spin. With our ley lines, you'll eat your words." Sage took his hand, and he tugged her up. With her aether, the melting pot of all elements, she possessed the ability to wield air, water, earth, and fire magic. But she only granted fire to her warlocks, the magic of all magics.

"Any warlocks catch your eye? Other than

Joshua?"

"You heard that BS?"

"Aspen made him the butt of several jokes making the rounds."

Sage cringed. Just what she needed. Another angry warlock hovering around. Speaking of, would Rafael Reyes return, or had the door slammed on his delectable rear? A wistful tweak on her heart proved how much she detested never seeing him again. She needed to track him down. After the festival, when normal life resumed. First, she needed to wake up and smell the roses. Every High Priestess in the region will badger her to form her protection team. Especially with the constant Helwig threats.

"I had my eye on one warlock." Movement in the gazebo sheltered by the trees and decorated in floral vines and fairy lights caught her attention. A young couple sucking each other's faces off sat on a marble bench. Wistfulness blossomed around her heart.

"Is he powerful? A good connection?"

More than she cared to blab to the world. "Very."

"Make a play for him. He'll boot everyone off your back until you find two more."

The door opened, and Aspen bounced onto the patio. She shut out the drama in the witch-house. "Those biotches won't let up."

Sage's spine arrowed straight. "Did the Helwigs leave?"

"Nope. The Council banished them, but allowed them to finish today's Council biz and attend the warlock lottery." Aspen hid a burp behind her hand and brushed her long, lustrous red hair behind her shoulders. Strawberries-and-rum-scented breath wafted from her. Sage had no plans to rat out her sister. The resulting hangover would be fitting punishment.

She spun her thoughts to more persistent matters. Thank the goddess Rafael had split, after all. Or else Zelda would snare him. Sage didn't want that fight on her scorecard.

"Better finish the meeting before we end up stomping down a revolution." Aspen headed to the door. "FY in your eye. Every High Priestess here's gonna force you to bag at least one warlock tomorrow."

Sage cringed. "How many available warlocks are there? I saw seven last night. Including The Tool." She traded wicked grins with Aspen.

"A dozen, give or take. They'll be on display"—she did air quotes—"at the party tonight. Maybe one or two will catch your eye, or another body part. Now get your rear in gear."

Sage plodded through the day to finish Council business. Unrestrained magic dwelled in every corner of the witch-house, the bulk stemming from the Helwig table. Lunch came and went, and the meeting ended at four o'clock.

Exhausted and jittery, Sage left, Ricky on one side and Aspen on the other. She plucked another drink from Aspen's hands and sucked down a gulp, gagged. "What god-awful concoction are you drinking now?" She jammed the glass into Aspen's grabby hand.

"Secret sauce."

"Geez, any more alcohol and you'll puke your guts out tonight."

"You'd know, right?"

"Bite me." Sage whacked Aspen's arm, jostling the glass in her sister's hand, the sticky drink sloshing over the sides. "I mean it. Cool it on the alcohol. I need your head clear."

Fake-pouting, Aspen dumped the drink in a box

planter of colorful summer annuals. "I'm just having fun."

"Have your fun. But be responsible." When did she start playing mother in this new reality?

"Can I go play with my itty-bitty friends now?" Aspen replied in a toddler's voice.

"Beat it." Sage waved her off. Aspen saluted her and jogged off toward the house.

"She's a good kid." Ricky guided her around a raised flagstone on the path cutting through the rear gardens.

"I don't want her repeating my stupid mistakes. Nor do I want to contribute to the delinquency of a dumb minor." Although Jessica was Aspen and Willow's legal guardian, Sage had adopted a quasi-parental role to her younger sisters. Another adulting item on her plate.

A group of Wilde warlocks caught Ricky's attention on the rear patio. "You okay if I check in? Everyone has their senses peeled for clues to our situation."

Sage bumped her elbow against his thick arm. "Go. I need a power nap, anyway."

C☆C C☆

Sage woke hours later, having missed dinner and the lighting of the bonfire. Twilight descended, swathing a purple hue over the sky. Mini lights, lanterns, and candles flickered in the backyard, like a million stars sprinkling the yard and perimeter woods. The celebration spilled out of the witch-house and onto the covenstead grounds, music and revelry ringing out into the night air.

Normally, she'd be queen of the party. The one

most likely to drink herself under the table, rip off her clothes, and dance naked in the meadow wearing only a floral crown. Not tonight. Although her election win was an unsurprising result of her family's long-standing authority in the witchworld, it was still worthy of a celebration. Yet, the heavy weight of her new duties dampened her already crappy mood.

She showered and slithered into a short, body-hugging dress, knee-high boots, and a tiny, leather half-jacket. Hair flowed free and lustrous. Time to make her expected appearance. Maybe she'd discover another unbonded warlock she'd missed last night. On her way out, she stooped to pick up a note Ricky had slid under the door. *Text me when you wake up. R.*

"Crap." She stuck her phone in the inner pocket of her boot, needing more alone time, at least on the short walk to the gathering. Who'd hurt her with a million witnesses watching?

A mad idea hit her brain, and she rushed down the hallway. It took her a half hour to reach the French doors leading to the patio after a myriad of witches stopped to congratulate her and chat. By the time she reached the open doors, peace lured her beyond the party. "Goddess, save me from this unnatural mood you dumped me in," she muttered.

Two witches sandwiched her in, clamoring for attention. "Sorry, I need to attend to Wilde matters. I'll catch up to you later." She rushed to the witch-house, greeting everyone who crossed her path, stopping shy of lingering for more chatting.

Bands of air rimmed by fire caged the unbonded warlocks at the back of the large room. Two water witches remained close to contain the fire from escaping and razing the barn. The warlocks strutted in various states of undress, all in good-natured fun.

Cognizant of her identity, they catcalled and whistled to her. They surged toward her, seeking her attention, but she only had a single-minded focus for two warlocks, both absent.

"Hey, guys! You're a feast for my eyes," she encouraged them, touching the biceps and abs of a couple preening like studs on a ranch. No magical insta-connections. Could she find a warlock to bond from this group? "We're missing two warlocks I met earlier today." And Joshua. Apparently, he'd escaped the cage. One could only hope he'd hit the road. "Anyone seen Rafael or Sammy? Helwigs brought them."

"Sammy's bonded. He returned to the Helwig covenstead." The familiar voice came from behind her.

Shoulders flinching, she spun around. "Hello, Joshua. Hope you're enjoying the festival." She nearly choked on her words. The stench of a brewery sailed off him, and he carried several longnecks.

"Not as much as I would've if you hadn't spread shit about me."

She smiled, attempting to set him at ease, but her smile ratcheted up a muscle tic in his jaw. "So sorry. You were the casualty of big ears and a bigger mouth. Join the group." She waved her arm at the gaggle of gorgeous men. "You'll find a witch." She moved on. "Has anyone seen an unbonded warlock by the name of Rafael Reyes?"

"What? The rest of us aren't good enough for you?" Joshua badgered, so close, his spit hit the side of her head.

Magic mounted inside her, and fire danced along her arm to her hand, tiny flames hardly perceptible to the naked eye. Three witches orbited the warlocks' cage, oohed and aahed over them, not paying attention to her other than to nod in respect.

"Joshua." Cringing inside, she touched his arm. A muscle jumped beneath her touch. "Don't you ever get up in my face," she gritted out. Sparks shot off her hand and scorched his flesh. He yelped and yanked his arm to his side. "See my healer about that sting."

The music swelled, and her head pounded. Magic bristling over her body, she snagged a fresh pale-yellow drink off the bar and escaped out the back door. No one followed, and she sped down a clear path into the woods toward her favorite bench fringed by trees and flowering shrubs. Lanterns containing battery-operated candles hung from the trees, illuminating the area and providing shadows to hide in. Gwyneira launched off her shoulder and took a perch on a tree behind the bench. She sat, the warmth from the June sun close to the horizon radiating off the cement.

"Hope Zelda picks that asshole." A titter slipped out, and she gulped her margarita on the rocks. "Ugh." The strong drink did nothing for her, and she dumped it out. An act unheard of before that day. "I've lost my freaking mind. Lost my way. What a way to start my new *job*." She kicked at a pine cone, and it thrashed into the bushes. "Do this, Sage. Do that. Bond a warlock or three." She flailed her arms in the air above her head.

"Do you always talk to yourself? Or are you talking to the trees?" The questions came from her left, and her head swung up. Excitement kick-started her heart into overdrive. Footsteps chased the voice, crunching on the gravel, until *he* stood in front of her.

Chapter 7

The most stunning sight of Rafael's crap-ass day, hell, his entire life, took his breath away. As full dark eclipsed the dregs of twilight, the shimmering lanterns lent Sage an ethereal glow he wanted surrounding them in a bubble together.

"Rafael," she breathed out his name. "You returned."

He cleared the frogs from his throat. He wasn't the type that got tongue-tied around a woman, but she brought out the worst—or the best—in him. "I never left."

Her slender fingers grasped her neck. "I thought you gave up on us."

"I hung on the fringes. Listened to the music, ate, drank. Watched."

She smiled. "So you're stalking witches now?"

"Just one." Head hanging, he shuffled his sneakers in the pea gravel on the pathway, pushing scattered rocks back onto the path. "You shouldn't be alone. Where's your warlock?"

"Gave him the slip. Besides, I'm *not* alone." She stepped toward him, and her scent washed over him, enticing and warm. "You're here."

"I'm not a warlock. Can't help you there," he said. Her wary gaze probed for signs and answers. "Why'd you dump your drink? Thought you're the badass party girl."

"You don't miss a trick, do ya?" Sage closed the distance between them. "I drink to slog through all the witchworld business. Because circumstances plunged me into a position of power way too soon. I drink to erase reality for a few hours." Her heat scorched him, but he wanted it touching him, needed it like air. "Tonight, I don't need alcohol. I want to feel everything... especially now."

She eased forward until a few inches separated them and pressed her palm on the center of his chest. His gut ignited, and he gasped, but didn't break contact. Her palm blazed through his chest, deep into his core and pulled that seething unnamed thing to the surface. Sparks shimmered off her hand, and he wasn't sure if she created the magic or if he did.

"What... what just happened?" he stammered.

"You *are* a warlock. I knew it!" Her hand slid up his chest, and her fingers trailed over his neck, leaving fire in their wake. She cupped his cheek. "You contain more power than I've ever seen in an unbonded warlock. Unique and all you."

He basked in her touch, shifted his head to the side and kissed her palm, his lips lingering against her soft, fiery skin.

"It's why I never left. I need to understand who I am." Anguish deepened his tone. "Zelda said she'd help me discover myself. It's why Sammy brought me to her." And just like that, he ruined the moment. Sage removed her hand, and a frigid wind blew off her and cooled the fire she'd left behind. Sparks dripped from her hand, and the wind scattered them like fireflies. "I suspect mentioning her name's not so cool."

"No. The Helwigs and Wildes have topped each other's shit lists for a century. Helwigs want to rule the entire witchworld. They ruled the West at one time, but succumbed to shenanigans that threatened everyone. The Wildes took charge and have remained in the power seat since."

Unsure how to respond, he soaked up the sight of her and her tropical scent, wishing they lay side by side on a deserted island, away from the madness.

"Look, Rafael. If you promised yourself to the Helwigs, I won't prevent you—"

"Whoa." He held up an open hand. "Back up the bus. I've made no promises. *She* made a claim on me, whatever that means. I need to understand why you all think I'm a warlock. But she wants me to quit my job, work and live at her covenstead. She made it sound like I'll be a kept man, no say in my life."

Tangible fury whisked around them as Sage released gusts of wind. Bands of white air glowed off her, floating from her spread palms. Her magic confused him. He'd heard she was a fire witch, not an air witch. Motion over her shoulder drew his attention to a fearless owl, watching them from a gnarled tree.

"If she claimed you, she'll fight newts and toads for you in the warlock lottery," Sage spat out the words like shards of glass.

He closed and opened his eyes. The bird still eyeballed him from its perch on a low tree branch. Sage folded her arms around herself, as if wrestling with the desire to touch him. God, he wanted it so damn much.

"Why's it called a lottery?" he asked, engaging in a safer topic.

Sage smiled her smile that sucked him in, one that belonged to him alone. "It's a loose term. A lottery requires consideration, prize, and a chance. Consideration is the goods and magic a witch will grant you if she chooses you. The warlock is the prize. A witch and the warlock both take a chance." She dropped her arms to her sides, her tension falling with them. "It is what it is."

"Got it." He revisited more pressing matters. Answers he needed first before he lost himself in Sage and lost his ability to think. "Who will Zelda fight against? Don't I get a choice? I mean, I can walk, right?" He crouched down, then sat on the gravel path, legs bent and chin resting on his right knee. "Your witchworld needs a Wiki." Sage towered over him and he didn't mind it, but he wanted her sitting next to him. He lifted up and tugged them both to the cement bench. "Do you mind? Can you stay a while?" The sparkle of her smile pierced him like an arrow straight to his heart.

She left her hand gloved in his. "I can stay as long as you want me to stay. I have a boatload to explain. Foremost, you absolutely have a choice. Somehow your friend Sammy suspected that you're a warlock. You won't possess actual powers until a witch bonds you, then you'll possess whatever magical element she wields." Sage toyed with the hem of her slick leather jacket that left little to the imagination. "Even if Zelda *claimed* you, you can choose any available witch on the prowl. Or walk. But understand this, you belong to the witchworld. That's the huge missing link from your life."

Absorbing her words, he squeezed her hand tighter, met her gaze, the lantern light catching on silver flecks in her emerald orbs.

"I need a warlock. I'm required to have three," she continued in a rush as though she needed to unload. "Ricky's ready to propose to his girlfriend, another witch. I'll need to break his bond. The Wilde Council may assign any random warlock to me. So I'm desperate." She flushed, and her heat hit him like a bonfire erupting in his stomach. "I mean, if I wasn't desperate, I'd still want you..."

The fiery boulder burst into fragments that shot through his bloodstream and straight to his throbbing dick. "So the Council could stick you with someone like Joshua?" he stuttered to diffuse his internal situation and grinned. She playfully slapped his arm. "Couldn't resist. I heard the story."

She buried her face on his shoulder. "Oh my goddess. I never meant the entire world to hear. I should've known better telling my bigmouth sister. Can we talk about anything else? Tell me who you are." She eased off the bench and stretched out on the path without a care in the world.

He lay down beside her and extended his arm to give her a pillow. "Rest your head on my arm." She did, snuggling close until their heads touched and her hand alighted on his thigh, practically singeing a hole through his jeans. He'd never met a woman who held such fire in her touch. Guess she truly was a witch and knew how to use her charms. Hell, they worked on him.

"What do you want to know?" he asked so gruff he thought he'd give away the lust barreling through him, if she hadn't already figured it out by the visible bulge. He had gone a year without the closeness of a woman, not wanting to risk involving another person in his tangled life. Even his prior occasional hit and runs wanted more from him than he could give.

"What's your favorite color?" Sage danced her fingers on the sleeve of his T-shirt.

"Gray."

"Wow. I've met no one who loved gray. Why?"

"Reminds me of old black-and-white photography. A neutral color, containing many shades that convey a depth, subtlety, and nuance." He shrugged, sending a ripple of movement through his body. "A versatile color with a wide range of emotions and impressions." He twisted a lock of her hair around his fingers and sniffed, savoring the faint fruity fragrance. "Goes with a lot of other colors too."

She shifted, and their gazes met and held. "Black is just black and white is just white. Gray's the middle where black and white meet, which colors your world."

He took her hand in his and settled their twined fingers on his thigh. "Right now, my favorite color is gold." He fingered strands of her silky hair.

She pinched the hem of his plain charcoal-gray T-shirt. A finger skimmed over his skin, and he quivered. "What do you do for a living? Where do you live? Oh, and are you single?" She whispered the last word as though she feared the answer.

An arrow pierced his heart. "I wouldn't be lying here, touching you if I wasn't single." Sparkles appeared in the air, glittering jewels in the sky. "If I bond a fire witch, can I do that?"

A hearty chuckle gushed from her. "That's a sample of what you'll be able to do. I'll show you more later."

"Will there be a later?" He held his breath.

She leaned across him, her breasts mashing

against his chest. Butterflies exploded in his rib cage as he pulled her closer, her softness pressing down the length of his body. The gentle touch of her hands on his face encouraged him, and he met her lips with his own. Her warm lips were inviting, and he deepened the kiss, falling under her spell. Time froze as they explored each other's mouths, and the world faded as they lost themselves in the moment. A first kiss that hinted at a future. Passion loaded the intense kiss, leaving him euphoric and wanting more, so much more. Air in short supply, they parted, foreheads touching. No matter how it all ended, he etched this moment forever in his memories.

"There will definitely be a later." Sage rolled off him, her head resting on his arm again. This time, she snuggled closer and twined her leg around his.

The night's first stars dotted the indigo canvas above. Starlight dappled the tops of the towering trees, glimmering like the fairy lights decorating the covenstead, creating an otherworldly atmosphere. He rested his cheek on top of her head. Lust beat at the doors of his sanity, and he hauled his thoughts back to the mundane. "I live in Santa Cruz in a shared house with two roommates. It's the only way we can afford it. I work for a security company, designing and installing security systems."

"Security? Hmmm. Now that my new role is official, a good security team sounds stellar."

"Damn straight. You have enough haters. You need to secure your property and house. I can set you up."

She rolled on her side and traced designs on his chest with her finger. "Well, we do have witch-style security."

"Oh. Yeah. Right." He paused, coughed to the side.

"So about—"

"Don't say her name." Groaning, she stretched her hand flat over his heart.

"What will happen if she or someone else claims me in the lottery?"

Sage lifted to scrutinize his face. "I'm claiming you. If you want, that is. You'll be the most powerful warlock in the West."

"Hell yes, I want you to. Zelda can go choke on her Botox." He waved his arm over their bodies. "After this, I can't deny there's a connection between us. More than magic. Or am I wrong?"

"You're not wrong." Sage dropped half on top of him again. "Goddess, Rafael. I've never met another warlock, or man, like you."

He clutched her tight and kissed the top of her head. "Ditto. I mean witch and woman."

She planted a kiss on his chest, her lips searing through his T-shirt. "Glad we're on the same page." Another kiss, so close to his heart, it skipped a beat. "Where are your parents? Why don't you know you're a warlock?"

"Grew up in the system."

"Oh. I'm sorry. You have witch blood in your family history somewhere. Well, at least you know now."

"But I don't know how to be a warlock."

"Don't worry. I think you'll catch on fast. Warlocks in my coven will teach you. And it's totally up to you, but there's an empty cabin on the property. Needs some TLC to make it habitable, but it's yours. Rent-free. We have the funds to upgrade it, just haven't gotten to that last one. No roommates, except the people who live and spend their days on the grounds. Again, no pressure. I'm not a Helwig. You'll have free rein among the Wilde coven."

His heart stuttered. He couldn't believe how his luck had changed. He needed a moment to digest. "Why all the cabins on the grounds?"

"Used to be a campground. My parents bought it, demolished the house and built the McMansion before I was born."

"I would've loved to have grown up here. I love the outdoors and hiking in the Santa Cruz hills. This sounds corny, but it's enchanted here."

"It's not corny. I feel the same. I've always thought it magical, and I never want to leave." Her finger danced another risky tango on his chest.

"My turn for questions. Why do all the Wilde witches keep the Wilde name? It wasn't your dad's last name, right?"

Her fingers reached the hem of his T-shirt and he sucked in his stomach in anticipation, but she didn't reach beneath. He exhaled a tinge of disappointment.

"Simple. Females in the witchworld keep their witch-heritage name. Anyone they marry has to suck it up." Her gaze flitted to his, gauging his reaction to such a momentous statement. Didn't bother him in the slightest.

"Do you know an owl's watching us from the tree behind us?" he asked. Her fingers trailed lower and reached dangerous territory. He stilled her hand. Not the time, not the place.

"That's Gwyneira." She waved at the owl and the owl winked a wide eye at her. "My familiar. She's watching you. If she sensed evil intent, she'd incapacitate you." Another small owl crawled out from beneath her sleeve. She flicked her hand, and the white owl flew off her fingers and alighted on his shoulder.

He felt a compulsion to close the short distance, only a strip of air between them. The owl flew back to Sage and disappeared beneath her dress.

"What did you feel?" she asked.

"Magic?" He squinted. "A tingle, a feeling like I had to get closer to you."

"That's my summoning familiar. I commanded her to compel you closer."

"Guess it's my lucky night that your owl didn't kill me." Gravel layered his words. "Can I kiss you again?"

"It *is* your lucky night. You can kiss me all you want."

As she rose up to meet his lips, people laughing and walking, or more like staggering, on the path alerted them to potential discovery. Cell phone lights bounced on the path and lit up the nearby trees. Sage and Rafael leaped up so fast they staggered into each other, missing knocking each other's head by a hair.

"Follow me." Before she darted into the woods to her secret path, Aspen called her name. They confronted her sister and a gaggle of witch friends. All hammered.

"Sage! Ricky's crawling out of his skin hunting you." Aspen slurred her words, wobbled between two witches equally unstable on their ridiculous platform heels. "Oh my goddess. Who's this hottie?" Her gaze slurped Rafael up from his feet to his hair. "Wait. You're that Rafael dude Zelda's yakking about. Thought you split."

"Aspen, shut it," Sage said under her breath. "Dial it down."

"Well, sis. You should be dancing and drinking. We're celebrating your ass too." Aspen teetered forward, and the girls caught her before she did a face-plant. They all burst out in giggles.

Rafael pivoted his body toward Sage. "Go. It's your day. The celebration's about you. Aren't you supposed to dance around the bonfire, chanting and holding candles with flower wreaths on your heads?" A smile toyed with his lips.

Sage had pulled Rafael from the brink of despair that night. He'd always known he differed from others, although no one ever expressed why. Foster families couldn't deal with his desperation to fit within the human world. He'd lived in group homes until booted out at eighteen. His background shaped this very moment, and he needed more time with Sage. Maybe a lifetime more.

"Not all's about me. It's our normal Summer Solstice festival," she replied. "And no, we don't do pagan dancing." She snickered. "Although we sprinkle ceremonial herbs in the bonfire for kicks, connect with nature by going into the forest, the ocean, or the meadow. All geared to feel the air against our bodies, the warmth of the sun seeping through us, creating a deeper connection to the earth, and letting the salt water cleanse us to prepare us for a new season."

"Guess I need to attend witch school."

Excitement in her eyes, she turned to her sister. "Text Ricky. Tell him I'm safe with a trusted warlock." On that note, she wrenched on Rafael's hand, and they sprinted down the path toward the mansion. "And quit drinking," she yelled over her shoulder.

"I'm sober as a judge," Aspen slurred and giggled.

Gwyneira flew above their heads, hooting and flapping its wings, guiding their way.

"Where're we going?" he asked. Sage stumbled on the uneven path cutting through the woods, and he caught her before her witch-air dove for the save. Landscape lights provided just enough illumination to avoid offing themselves.

"To my bedroom. No one'll bother us there."

Rafael screeched to a standstill, hauling Sage into his arms to keep her from falling. "You said you never take warlocks to your bedroom."

She linked her arms around his neck and smashed her boobs against his chest. Instant hard-on. She rubbed herself against him right where it counted. "They're witch-style one and dones. I didn't want to sully my bedroom with that business."

His heart galloped. *What was she saying?* "I'm not a one and done?" he asked, breath lodging in his throat as he waited for her answer.

"I don't need to sex it up with you. Goddess, I'm dying to. But your magic is so strong, I've already sensed your power and abilities. For once in my life, I need slow. I need the burn of touching, kissing, and getting to know one another first. You'll be the first and only warlock ever to grace my bedroom."

Chapter 8

Gwyneira swooped down from the sky, startling Rafael. He batted at the owl's wings flapping at his head. The familiar landed on Sage's shoulder, evaporated to ink, and slithered under her dress.

"Where'd it go?" Rafael spun in a circle seeking her familiar.

Sage plucked the neckline of her dress aside, revealing Gwyneira's white wings. "Once I bond you, you'll see a familiar shift from real to tattoo. And you'll have an owl familiar as your own, who can guide your magic in certain ways."

He traced the tattoo on her neck, his gentle fingers inciting a hormonal jig in her southern parts. "I like the sound of that. *Once you bond me.*"

"Will you accept?" She gloved his hand on her skin, needing his touch to breathe.

"Let's hit up your bedroom, and I'll let you know." He chuckled and brushed his mouth over her lips. He clutched her hand again, and they resumed their trek to the side yard to avoid the partiers.

An almost hypnotic herb-laced wood smoke perfumed the air, giving more impetus to Sage's actions. She guided him into the garage and through the kitchen, winking at the kitchen staff, her index finger cutting up her lips to request their silence. She snatched a tray of mixed appetizers, and Rafael grabbed a half-empty bottle of Bordeaux wine and two plastic cups. They zipped up the back staircase to her bedroom.

Rafael opened the door and stepped over the threshold. He jolted back, fumbling with the wine bottle before it fell to the floor. "Whoa."

Sage's jaw dropped. "It's warded from intrusion by magicals. Try that again."

Again, he stepped a toe over the threshold, and an invisible wall thrust him into the hallway.

"Holy hell. Your magic's potent. My ward shouldn't have impeded an unbonded warlock or non-magical from entering." Adrenaline popped in her blood. "What do you feel?"

Rafael scratched his head. "Felt like a burning mattress forcing me out."

"No, I mean, how do you feel inside?" Sage held up a finger for him to wait. She uttered the spell to kill her protective ward and wiggled her fingers toward the doorway to dispel the magic. "Get in here." She set the appetizers on a small accent table between two cushiony chairs in front of the large window overlooking the backyard. He shut and locked the door. "Smart man." Grinning, she took the wine and cups from him, set them by the food.

Appreciation lit up Rafael's eyes as he perused the large bedroom and the king-size bed. A dozen earth-tone pillows decorated the cream, gray, and pale sage comforter. "Not much different from my normal. Like something sizzling inside me. Since I've tasted your magic, I know it's magic waiting for a witch to tap. Seems like fire, air, water, earth all rolled in one."

Sage sagged down on one of her cushiony arm chairs. "It sounds like—" She stopped herself from saying "her aether." Too soon to give up all the goods on her magic. "You need a powerful witch to uncork your magic." She picked up a cucumber and cream cheese sandwich and absently chewed it, handed one to Rafael, who chose a meatier appetizer instead.

"Are you that witch?" He chomped on a handful of pigs in a blanket. Simple fare for the festival.

She fake-sneered, flicked a finger in the air. Appetizers flew out of his hand and floated in the air. "Want more of that?"

"No! I'm starving." He laughed. She floated the food back to him, and he caught them in his cupped hands. They ate and drank in companionable silence for a few minutes, until Rafael asked, "But I'd kill to do stuff like that. How 'bout you bond me tonight?"

Sage's heart thudded in her chest. Her shock and absolute joy on the best day of her life swamped her. She scrunched her face and groaned. "I hate to even put this out there. No. You need to absorb everything you've learned today. I *will* bond you. No question. But I also want to make it special." She lowered her pitch seductively. "I may include sex."

Rafael choked up a weeny bit. "Then let's fucking do it now," he croaked out and guzzled his wine.

"Can we just hang tonight? It's been a long-ass day."

"I know, babe. I'm kidding."

Sage didn't miss the word "babe." He'd said it so natural and heartfelt. No doubt Rafael could be her

First Warlock, the one who'd rule by her side, her right hand. Her forever warlock.

She moved to sit on her bed and pulled her boots and jacket off, then lay back, bolstering her head on her toss pillows. She patted the bed beside her. "I don't mind if we get more comfortable and fool around, though."

Sage and Rafael tumbled into their comfortable and calm private world. They talked, touched, laughed, and most definitely kissed until the early morning hours when Sage fell asleep wrapped in Rafael's arms.

C★C★C★

Sage awoke the next morning to find Rafael watching her sleep, a grin morphing his already handsome face into gorgeous territory, more so with his tousled bed-hair.

"Are your eyes stalking me?" She hid a yawn and her fuzzy morning breath behind her hand. For once, she didn't care that her makeup and hair resembled Beetlejuice.

"Can't help it. You're so damn beautiful." He feathered a kiss across her forehead.

"Good morning to you too." Her hand accidentally brushed his steely erection hiding in his black briefs— they'd stripped down to their underwear in the early morning hours—and she jerked her hand to her hip. "Sorry. I wasn't trying to tease."

"Tease all you want." But he put an inch or two of space between their lower regions. "Last night, this morning—" He choked up. "Is all this real?"

"Magical?" Her eyebrows arched. "I keep pinching myself."

"Beyond magical." He nuzzled her neck, sending goosebumps across her skin.

Avoiding his erection, Sage snuggled against Rafael's firm, muscular body one last moment before crawling out of bed. One more day to adult, then she could take a breather before her future submerged her.

"I'll grab you a toothbrush." She slipped on a short, silky robe and escaped the room before Rafael's body enticed her to remain in bed all day.

She gathered guest toiletries from the hall bathroom and snagged a newish, clean gray T-shirt from the hallway of abandoned clothes. The Wildes always enjoyed overnighter guests and had designated the cabinet a free-for-all of left-behind items.

Hands full, she bumped into a staggering Aspen in the hallway outside her bedroom door. Her hair hung in strings and she wore pasty like a zombie. "Aspen tree. How you feeling?"

"Stop." Aspen covered her ears. "Don't screech at me." Her bleary gaze raked over the toiletries in Sage's hand, and her head inched up. "Zelda has already claimed Rafael. Don't start anything with him. We need to let the emotions die down."

"It's already started. I can't *not* make a claim on him."

"You're falling for him?"

"Already fallen," Sage replied.

"Oh my goddess." Aspen cupped her mouth. "Today's not gonna be a good day."

"Not for Zelda."

"Not for *you*." Aspen brushed past Sage and rushed into the bathroom.

"Not for you either." Sage snickered and strode to

her bedroom, hoping to find Rafael still in bed. She needed another snuggle. What a fantastic, exquisite night.

An empty bed and water spraying in her shower built for at least two met her senses. Did she dare? She stood outside the ajar bathroom door, bit her bottom lip. Decided he was too alluring. If she didn't make a full-day appearance at the festival, someone would release flying monkeys down upon her. Plus, she had to skate through the warlock lottery and make her sole choice. The heavenly man standing naked in her bathroom.

Averting her gaze from the shower, she dumped the toiletries and T-shirt on the expansive vanity and called downstairs for breakfast. The kitchen staff provided a breakfast spread in the dining room and the witch-house for the overnighters, but she wanted more alone time with Rafael before facing the masses. Not knowing what foods he liked—they hadn't discussed favorite foods—she ordered multiple items for him.

The shower door clicked open and thunked shut. Sage waited to give him time to dry off before approaching the bathroom.

"Use anything you need," she said through the crack in the door.

"I was waiting for you to join me," he tantalized.

"No you weren't." She laughed. "But I thought long and hard about it."

"Don't use the word *hard*, babe. I'm in a state of perpetual hard around you."

The word "babe" again softened her heart. She jabbed the door open. He stood in front of her vanity, facing the door. His chestnut-dark hair slicked back, water glistening on his bare chest, dripping to the smattering of hair arrowing down to the top of the towel wrapped around his waist, showing clear evidence of his *hard.*

"You called me 'babe.'" She touched her palm to his damp chest.

"Sorry, it slipped." He covered her hand with his. "I've never called another girl that. Not sure where it came from."

Heat pooled in her lower region. "Cool. I like it."

They remained in the moist, warm bathroom for a moment, taking each other in until text messages blew up Sage's phone from the bedroom.

"Give me a few and the bathroom's all yours." He picked up the T-shirt. "How'd you know Led Zeppelin's my favorite band?"

"The only gray shirt in the lost and found. But now I know your favorite band." Her phone kept dinging. "Crap, I gotta check my texts."

Ricky wanted to know what warlock was protecting her after Aspen's cryptic message to him last night. She texted: *Don't worry. I'm safe. In bedroom.*

He texted: *I know you're in your bedroom. Who's with you?*

She responded: *Tell you later. Dad!*

She'd missed enough of the festival, and witches had been hunting her down last night. Most wanted to catch up on life, others wanted to discuss witchworld progression before the festival ended. Not ready to share Rafael with the world, she'd remained cryptic, stating she had a headache and needed to rest.

She texted Aunt Jessica: *Be down soon. Feel fantastic.*

"Trouble?" Rafael wrapped her in his arms from

behind, resting his chin on her shoulder. "God, I feel like I've come home. You're uber comfortable to be with. Sorry if that's too much to hear. I just—"

Sage pivoted in his arms, rested two fingers over his lips. "It's exactly what I want to hear."

And he kissed her, his minty-fresh mouth hungry, his lips soft and firm at once. She twined her arms around his neck, feeling the warmth of his skin against hers. His arms wrapped tight around her, a haven so unlike anything she'd ever experienced. She pressed so close to him, like two halves of a whole reunited after a long, difficult separation. The kiss deepened, and Sage was drowning in Rafael, until breathless and they separated.

"As much as I want to kiss you all day, I can't shirk my duties any longer." She punctuated her words with quick pecks on his mouth.

"I know." He adjusted the crotch of his jeans. "This bonding thing better happen soon."

"You're cocky," she teased.

He thrust back his head and groaned. "Don't say 'cock.' You're killing me. And damn straight I'm cocky. Can you say this *wasn't* fate? I was meant to come to your covenstead this Summer Solstice. You're the reason I couldn't leave when I ghosted you yesterday. Something, *you*, grounded me here."

A knock banged the door and broke the spell. Before Sage answered it, she said, "The goddess works in mysterious and wondrous ways. Everything yesterday and this morning that drove us together happened for a reason. Right time, right place, the stars, moon, and sun aligned for this perfect moment in time." She stroked his arm, loving the firmness and strength beneath her fingers. "Now I gotta go rule the rest of the day. Open the door and eat the breakfast waiting in the hallway. I need to shower and beautify myself."

"I doubt you can improve upon this." He wanded his hand the length of her body.

"Give me a half hour and you'll change your tune." She added an extra sway to her hips and sauntered into the steamy bathroom.

Chapter 9

The phrase "love at first sight" sunk Rafael. He'd never believed in insta-love. Until he'd met Sage Wilde. He'd kissed her one last time in her bedroom until her lips were plum and plump. They'd decided to keep their night together under wraps.

Avoiding people, he escaped down the rear stairway of the crazy-huge Wilde mansion and thanked the kitchen staff for the best breakfast he'd ever eaten. Sage assured him the kitchen witches were discreet. Despite his stuffed stomach, he helped himself to another mug of gourmet coffee and lingered at a semi-hidden corner of the back patio, his shoulder propped against a pillar. A man could get accustomed to the plentiful food at the Wilde covenstead, the beautiful scenery, the total picture. And seeing Sage every day.

His gaze wandered to the people peppering the lawn and hiking the paths from the meadow, witch-house, and the mansion. A carnival atmosphere. Sage explained how the California covens rotated hosting the Summer Solstice festival every three years.

He peered beyond the yard into the woods at the line of cabins trailing to the meadow, and the other cabins stretching through the trees on the opposite side of the thicket. What did it mean to be a warlock, the western High Priestess's right hand? Or to live on this kickass property? They had talked little about their future, but the excitement coursing through his blood had forever changed him. For once in his life, he belonged somewhere with people who understood him, with a gorgeous woman who'd become the brightest star in his world.

On the other side of the lawn, Zelda and her entourage gathered in a group. When her eagle eyes spied him, he nodded in greeting. Her expression remained intractable, her movements jerky. A step beyond her regular resting bitch face. She flicked her hand and several warlocks disbursed, including Sammy. Man, he needed to thank Sammy for helping to make yesterday the best day of his life once he'd swallowed his lame fears and hopped on board the witchworld train.

Sammy rushed toward him, a grimace turning his smile upside down. "Dude, thought you left."

"Planned to. Decided to chill here instead." He set his empty mug on a patio table. "What bug crawled up Zelda's ass? By the looks of it, she's prepping to go apeshit."

Sammy shifted his weight, his gaze skittering away from Rafael's face. "Beats me. Guess she slept in the wrong bed."

Unease wound through Rafael's full stomach. "I wanted to thank—" Before he finished his sentence, several pairs of feet scuffled behind him, and a full hood landed over Rafael's head. "Hey! What the fuck?" Someone muffled his mouth, and he recognized a band of witch-air. They half carried and walked him to the side of the garage out of view of potential witnesses.

Sammy leaned in close. "Don't fight it," he murmured. "It's a warlock hazing ritual. You'll be fine."

Silent, his captors wrenched his arms behind his back and tied his wrists in another air band. Rafael struggled against the arms shuttling him forward. He wasn't fine. Sage didn't tip him off to any hazing ritual. On the verge of hyperventilating, he forced himself to concentrate on just filling his lungs with air. A foster brother once tried to smother him with a pillow in his sleep, and this act felt identical. Ever since the incident, he'd loathed having his head and mouth covered. Feared never coming out alive. Kicking and trying to shout through his gag, he fought off his captors.

Knocking him around with quiet deliberation, they shoved him onto the carpeted floor in the rear of an SUV or van. A warlock slipped his hand in Rafael's back pockets and nicked his phone and wallet.

Another warlock clambered beside him, and the engine rumbled to life. He checked his breathing, tried to deal with the red-hot pokers stabbing his middle, spearing through his untapped magic. Too bad his magic remained dormant, or he'd blast these assholes to the North Pole with a one-way ticket.

"Dude. Take it easy," Sammy said in a low voice. "It'll be over soon."

The cargo hold smelled fresh, as though used for transporting people, not gym bags or pets. Or dead bodies. It gave him a skosh of hope. A few moments later, Rafael's heartbeat steadied and his breathing leveled out. He railed at his so-called friend behind the hood and gag, to no avail. Rafael had to ride it out and conserve his strength for the right moment. Evil permeated this bullshit act, and he didn't believe for a second it was a hazing. He lay on his side to keep from leaning on his hands and risk them falling asleep. Once the bastards untied his wrists, he wanted full use because he was raring to bash some heads.

He'd met Sammy three months ago through one of his roommates, and they'd become fast friends. Yesterday, when they'd passed through the Helwig covenstead's gates, the sound of metal squeaking against metal had echoed in Rafael's ears, but didn't suppress Sammy's words when he'd unloaded his shocking warlock status. Sammy's head was first on the chopping block.

They drove for about twenty minutes when the screech of wrought-iron gates sliding open confirmed his theory. The Helwig covenstead. *I knew that bitch is calling the shots.*

Sage had given him an earful about the animosity between the two covens throughout the decades. Rafael had sensed evil in Zelda from the jump, and didn't care for her attempts to dominate him, a far cry from Sage's warm and open acceptance. He wanted nothing to do with the Helwigs on principle alone.

The vehicle engine shut off. The doors opened and slammed shut, rocking the vehicle and knocking his head against the back seats.

"Don't fight the process, dude," Sammy said again under his breath as if he didn't want the other warlocks to hear.

It took everything in Rafael to ignore his backstabbing friend when he wanted to blast him a new one. No sense in engaging him again. He was toast on the friendship front.

The rear doors opened, hands gripped his ankles and dragged him out of the cargo. He wanted to fight tooth and nail, but again resisted. They weren't trying to hurt him, and puzzlement battled the anger in his head. The feeling that Zelda wanted to remove him from the warlock lottery for her own selfish purposes refused to subside inside his churning stomach.

Several dudes—he assumed warlocks—guided him inside a building. He swore if this went assbackwards, he'd go full medieval on whoever was involved. They steered him down a staircase and through a doorway.

Someone killed the spell on his air muzzle and plucked the hood off. "What the hell is going on?" He glared at the warlocks, three he recognized from the Helwig crowd. No Sammy in sight. The small, windowless room built from cinderblock with a bare cement floor mirrored a jail cell.

"We have orders to hold you until Ms. Helwig returns." The leader dangled the hood from his hand. The other two took up defensive stances, legs spread and arms crossed over their chests, barring the door.

"This isn't a warlock hazing. It's a fucking abduction." Rafael's untapped magic boiled fiery bubbles in his gut, rising and popping like a severe case of indigestion.

The two wingmen laughed. "Good one," Tall, Blond, and Skinny squeaked out. "We don't haze warlocks." He cracked his knuckles as if gearing up for a fight. "We might make an exception for you, though."

"No," Leader Dude said. "Zelda said to make him comfortable. This is all the comfort you get." He grabbed Rafael roughly, and with one swift motion, released the spell on his shackles. Blood gushed to his stinging wrists. The warlocks backed out of the small dank room, locking Rafael inside.

He rubbed his wrists, flexed his taut arms and searched the room for a weapon or a way out. A twin bed, a sink, and toilet behind a curtain comprised the cell. At least they'd given him toilet privacy, more than most prisons. He whacked the curtain, almost pulling it from the rods dangling from the ceiling.

"Son of a bitch." Rafael pounded on the steel door. After working out his frustrations on the door, he paced the tiny room, his fists curling and uncurling at his sides. Would Sage search for him? Had he made a big enough impression on her for a future together in any way, shape, or form? Or would she cut and run and find another warlock to bond? Did he even want to join the witchworld and learn about himself in exchange for being treated like a tool? His mind churned with what-ifs.

At least an hour rolled by before he heard keys jangling and scraping the door. The lock clicked, and the door opened. Zelda Helwig parked it on the threshold, toting a wicked smile that truly personified a witch hag, absent her decrepit broomstick and nasty flying monkeys.

He sprang up from his perch on the thin mattress atop a crap-ass daybed and gave Zelda the hairy eyeball. "You can't hold me here. It's called kidnapping." Warlocks behind her blew gale force winds around her that shoved him backward onto the bed. It stole his breath for a few seconds until he blocked the air from hitting his face.

"It rather appears that I *am* holding you here." Her smile didn't budge.

"What do you want from me?"

"You came to me, if I recall." She swished her arms up. "I'm giving you the world you've craved."

A headache brewed behind his eyes. "I'm good. I've changed my mind." Lies rolled to the surface. If he wanted to learn anything more, he'd learn it from Sage. "Let me leave now."

"No takebacks. Time to play this out. You contain huge amounts of untapped power, and I can unleash it. Then you'll beg to remain at my side."

Air in the room became murky over Zelda as she shrouded herself in a bubble. A strange smell wafted from the air vent in the ceiling, permeating the room. Acidic on one hand, sweet and tangy on the other. Cupping his palm over his nose, dizziness overcame him. He faltered and his butt hit the top of the mattress.

"What are you doing to me?" he slurred, every muscle and bone in his body floating on air.

Zelda eased closer, the bubble of air preceding her. He tried to touch her, but the solid air pushed against his hand. Crouching down in front of him, she cupped a hand to his cheek, and he couldn't raise a finger to stop her. "Think of the possibilities of being bonded to the most powerful witch in the region."

She flicked her hand. Her two warlocks left and shut the door behind them. "Don't worry. I won't hurt you. I won't touch you if you prefer. We can proceed without sex. But sex always makes everything better." She licked her tongue up his cheek, massaged his rising erection. An erection he fought to contain, but he'd lost control of his reality, his entire mind and body, even his soul. Foreign commands dictated his every thought and movement, and he was powerless to resist.

"Do you want me to bond you, Rafael Reyes?" She pressed a kiss to his lips and then kissed her moonstone ring. "You must verbalize your consent."

A fissure formed in his confused mind. It screamed "NO" at him. But it didn't match the words rising to the forefront, or the directives his mouth and hands threatened to take.

Leaning forward and digging his hand through the dense air shrouding her, he cupped his hands around her cheeks, pressed his lips to hers until that tiny dissenting vote in his head stabbed his brain. He kissed the moonstone ring she held up to his lips, the stone warm and inviting. Sharp pains in his skull forced him to pull back.

"It's okay." Zelda rose to her full height. "Words are enough. Until later."

The strange conflicting scent overpowered him, lured him to fill his lungs to capacity. The muddle lessened in his head, smothering that dissenting nag, until a new clarity chased the fog out to sea.

Slowly, he lifted his heavy head, the weight of it causing a crick to form in his neck. "Yes. I want you to bond me. I agree to your dominion, and I swear fealty to you and the Helwig coven."

Chapter 10

Delight splashed through Sage. She grinned like a besotted idiot as she entered the witch-house after being summoned by nearly every witch in her coven. She didn't expect to see Rafael until after lunch. The morning gave the witches more time to peruse and grill the unbonded warlocks, and she didn't want anyone else laying claim to Rafael. The visuals of his to-die-for body lingered in her mind, and she couldn't wait to see him again for the warlock lottery.

"Sage!" Jessica shouted in admonishment mode from across the room. "You need to make a choice." Witches and warlocks jammed the corners in small groups, chitchatting and eating breakfast before the final festival events. Jessica handed her the clipboard with the unbonded warlock names.

"I know, I know. I've picked one," Sage replied.

"What!" Jessica squealed a little too eager. "You found a warlock to bond?" Jessica clenched Sage's arm, her eyes widening mischievously. "Don't tell me you're bonding Joshua."

"Hell to the no way." She examined the list. Multiple High Priestesses claimed most warlocks, which meant each witch had to convince a warlock to choose her over another. Three-quarters down the list, two warlocks had one witch name beside his. Helwig. No one ever wanted to battle Zelda. She always won. One name was Joshua. *Good luck with that.* The last name, Rafael, had only Zelda vying for him. A smile kicking up the corners of her lips, she seized the pen from Jessica and wrote her name on Rafael's line.

Jessica's fingertips dug into Sage's arm. "It'll end in disaster if you fight her on this. Choose another warlock or wait. We can stall the Council on forcing you to select one today." Jessica kept talking as if Sage wasn't shaking her head. "He's not worth it, is he?" Resignation layered each word.

"Aunt Jessica." Excitement barreling through her, she said in a rush, "He's worth more than all these warlocks lumped together. We connected and spent all night together." Sparks flew off her fingers and drizzled to the floor. "We're meant for each other. The way my magic connected to him was surreal. His untapped power is tangible."

"So you two had sex?" Jessica squinted.

"Goddess knows I wanted to. We connected on so many levels unrelated to the witchworld. I didn't need sex to tap his power." Rafael's aura differed from anything Sage had ever seen. Since he had an uber powerful aura, she knew it killed him not to grasp everything happening to his body. He needed a witch to bond him before he tripped off the rails.

Startled, Jessica shook her head, her earrings tinkling as she stepped back.

Ben rushed over, his hand settling on his wife's

shoulder. "What's wrong? Where's Ricky?"

"We're fine." Sage patted the air for him to dial it down. "Ricky's investigating a lead on my attack."

"What are you saying, Sage?" Jessica whispered. "Did your aether connect with him?"

"Yes... I think it did. It was surreal."

"Who? We need him in the coven. The aether connection's a game changer." Ben leaned forward as though to press his words onto Sage. He trailed his index finger down the list until it rested on Sage's sole selection, and groaned. "Will he pick you over Z?"

"Yep. We already discussed it. He knows Zelda has no claim on him, despite her lies to the contrary."

"Where's the warlock now?" Ben searched the room over their heads. "Don't see him. In fact, I don't recall seeing him at all."

"Zelda scared him off yesterday. But he remained on the fringes." Sage picked at her fingernails. "He's hanging outside. He'll be here for the lottery."

"Not good enough. Ricky and I need to meet him," Ben ordered. "Call him. This is a make-or-break decision on both your parts going up against the Helwigs."

Sage threw up her hands, more sparks dripping from her fingers. "Okay. Okay." She dug her phone out of her jeans pocket. She'd dressed casual on the last day of the festival. A chill lingered in the air, hence the long pants versus summer shorts. Her call to Rafael rolled to voicemail, and she left a message, then texted him: *Ben and Ricky want to meet you ASAP. Come to the witch-house.*

While waiting for a response, she greeted the witches who thanked her and Jessica for a wonderful festival. Fifteen minutes of radio silence later, her anxiety flew off the charts. A tapeworm of paranoia wound through her belly. Jeopardizing new relationship cling-on status, she texted Rafael several more times. More ghosting. As she turned to stand at the podium, a strange draw on her aether left her gasping. She teetered, caught herself against the podium.

"You okay?" Ricky rushed up behind her, arriving for his security duties. Although an entourage of Wilde witches and warlocks surrounded her, she needed her warlock in case the lottery went sideways.

"Yeah. Tripping over my own feet." She forced out a laugh, while someone carved a knife through her internal magic, leaving an aching hollow. A hole devoid of future, hope, and promise. *What the what?* All eyes in the room shifted to her, and her time to freak slipped into the ether.

Fighting against the crater inside her, she forced the words and motions for the morning's blessing. Other witches in the room joined in for their parts, sprinkling herbs, and lighting candles at the four points of the compass to signify air, water, fire, and earth.

The last event arrived, and the witch-house filled to the brim. The lottery represented a fun escape to watch the witches bicker over unbonded warlocks and the warlocks getting their rocks off on decisions that guaranteed a profound effect on their life. Witches had a last half hour to spend with the unbonded warlocks to confirm their choices.

Anticipation pervaded the witch-house. They'd cleared out the four long tables and set rows of chairs and smaller round tables in their place that filled up fast.

"Anything?" Jessica asked.

"No. I'm worried. He should be here for the

lottery." Sage gnawed on her bottom lip. "The Helwigs aren't here either."

"Are you sure your connection was as strong as you think?" Jessica asked.

"Maybe he played you." Aspen elbowed inside their huddle, rocking a lovely shade of green. "You know, just to screw your brains out. Hit and run."

Sage whacked her sister's arm, a tad harder than playfully. "Shut it. We didn't have sex," she gritted out. "I swear to the goddess, I'm not making shit up."

Mollified, Aspen hugged her sister's arm, more for her own stability than Sage's support. "Just yanking your chain. Sorry."

"Honey, you need to prep for the lottery," Jessica encouraged. "I'm sorry about Rafael. Maybe he needs time to sort out his head. If he doesn't return, we'll find the right warlock for you."

Sage left their huddle, her senses sweeping one corner of the room to the next and everywhere in between. Still no Rafael. Had she imagined the incredible night they'd spent together? The joy surging through her? Had he led her on? Questions swirled in her bewildered mind. Had she imagined a break in her aether, a scattered piece of herself that already belonged to Rafael?

C⋆C⋆C⋆

Rafael lifted off the bed, his languorous body barely able to obey the commands his brain spoon-fed it. Surely the witch had spelled him. How else would his body betray him? Hope floated in his mind as a few memories lingered. The radiant blonde witch. What was her name? He struggled with the recollection but it slipped away. Guess it didn't matter. Zelda Helwig promised to show him what he'd missed all his life. She promised him a future of knowledge and power. So what if she wanted him to quit his job and move to Scotts Valley? So what if the witch wanted him in her bed? Although way older than any other woman he'd slept with, she wasn't bad looking. It's not like he planned to marry her. Plus, she promised him a job on her covenstead. But the idea of being a quasi-kept man didn't sit well. He fisted his hands. Everything else in his mind fell by the wayside.

"Come, Rafael." Zelda kissed him on the mouth, her thin lips glacial. "Follow me to my spelling circle."

He marched behind her up the stairs to a large room. A painted pentagram decorated the polished cement floor. She guided him to the center of the pentagram and placed unlit candles at each point. Thick, pliant air seemed to imprison him in a cocoon. He listlessly raised his right arm an inch, and the air slapped against him, curtailing his motions.

"Careful, Rafael. I've bound you in air. I'll join you in a moment." She lit the candles one by one, reciting words Rafael had a difficult time hearing let alone digesting.

The air shroud wavered and thinned. Zelda appeared next to him, holding two candles. She handed one to him, the flame dancing from the air sifting around them. She took his free hand in hers.

"Recite each line after me." She voiced the bonding spell, words Rafael didn't grasp.

By rote, he repeated each line after she uttered it. At the end, Zelda blew out her candle and motioned for him to do the same. As the flames sputtered out, a sharp, stabbing sensation ripped through his insides, like someone had thrown a shattering bowling ball into his middle. Fire broiled his internal walls, and he staggered against Zelda. She caught him, but his weight slumped them both to the floor, witch-air cushioning their fall.

A squiggly, rushing sensation up his right forearm left him gaping at the bobcat tattoo blending over his skin. Zelda's bonding familiar.

Three warlocks joined them, helping them stand and guiding Rafael to a seat on a wooden dining room chair. For the first time, he noticed no cushions or couches in her living room. All the chairs and benches were wood or cement, absent all the comforts of the Wilde home. *Wilde?* Fruitlessly, he waggled his head to dislodge lost memories trying to cut through the fog.

Every fiber of his being sizzled. An airy sensation flooded his middle, giving him the consuming need to disburse it somehow. Fire rimmed it, but didn't expand. He needed more magic to fill the voids. Adrenaline pumped through his languid body. Toting a newfound purpose, a sense of hope for the future energized him. The witch-air dislodged incoherent memories. He tried to study them, but his body forced him to concentrate on the sensations creating havoc in every cell of his body.

"You're feeling my magic, Rafael," Zelda explained. "As you learn to use my air and fire, it'll normalize."

Shock zinged through his chest. The witch had awakened that sleeping giant inside him. He couldn't say she'd awakened all of it, but his internal eyes had blinked. Concentrating, he stood and forced a ball of air to roll to his open palm.

"You're a natural." Zelda beamed and clapped. "You'll gain in power as you learn to use my magic. We can take over the witchworld." An evil, eager tone accompanied her words, and with an unnatural exhilaration Rafael believed them.

"It's incredible." Gravel layered his voice, and his eyes bulged in awe.

Zelda withdrew a heavy silver chain from her billowy blouse pocket. A carved, silver bobcat pendant hung from it. She looped the shiny chain around his neck. "You're a Helwig coven member. Always wear it." Then she tied a leather, beaded bracelet around his wrist. "The beads are a conduit which will help your magic."

He inspected the trinkets she'd gifted him, tracing the bobcat design.

"Toss the ball of air."

"I don't want to damage anything." As he focused on the growing, opaque ball on his palm, an ache formed behind his eyes and they fogged over. He stopped concentrating and the weird sensations retreated.

"Don't worry, dear." She scrubbed her hands together. "As time goes by, I'll feed you more power to bolster your abilities, including my fire magic. Let's go slow. Think and say the word 'fly.'"

Spinning on his heel, he turned to an empty corner of the room and commanded, "Fly!"

The air ball soared off his hand to the far side of the room and blasted an empty ceramic vase off a black coffee table. The vase crashed to the floor in a million shards of silver ceramic and pinged the floor and walls.

Zelda clapped. "Oh, dear goddess. You're amazing."

"Sorry." Rafael moved across the room, his stride slow. He swished his foot over the floor, sweeping the shards into a pile.

"Leave it for my cleaning staff." Heading toward the front door, she motioned him to follow. "We must return to the festival."

Two warlocks joined them, and they loaded up in Zelda's gray SUV.

Everything inside Rafael turned airy. The small amount of witch-air he'd blasted didn't make a dent in the magic prodding the gates of his insides.

Zelda faced him in the back seat. "Do you see your potential now?"

The elation in his heart felt like a caged bird, desperate to be released. "Yes. Thank you, Zelda."

She leaned closer, propping her hand on his knee, and she forced his head closer to her. She kissed him, her lips imparting no warmth, only a cold desolation. Repulsed, he didn't respond to the kiss, battling the motherly vibe toting a major ick factor.

Instead, all his desire focused on the beast she'd awakened inside him. When would his entire body awaken? When would those insidious memories banging the crypts of his mind pop through the doors? Would the heat of the bracelet stop burning his wrist and kill that intoxicating odor he'd smelled in the small room and now on the beads?

Chapter 11

Sage delayed the lottery until various witches excited for the show badgered her to begin. Some were raring to hit the road after three days of meetings, ceremonies, and parties.

How'd a night and morning of absolute bliss morph into a hot poker stabbing her middle? Her intuition never kicked her in the butt. Despair caused the connection she'd shared with Rafael to splinter every moment he didn't appear. A bereft and decimated ice formed around her, despite the heat of her witch-fire.

After sweeping the room one last time, she caught Ricky's eye. He lifted his hands, let them fall. One last fruitless check on her cell phone and she tapped two fingers on the microphone. The sound thumped to the open beam ceiling and quieted the excited tittering. The last standing witches took their seats. She needed this stupid-ass lottery over. She had chosen no other warlock, and she no longer had a stake.

"Greetings." She bestowed a smile she didn't feel

on the unbonded warlocks standing to her left. Although the warlocks preened for attention, a nervousness rode the air. A new, exciting, and sometimes perilous life lay ahead of them.

Sage addressed the young men. "May the goddess bless you all with enlightenment in the choices you make. This role will change your life. It's a great honor for a High Priestess to choose you to join her coven. You'll enjoy a long life with magic, acceptance of your identity in the world at large, and a place to call home. You may find love"—she nearly choked on the word— "or a great companionship, as well as many new friendships. *You will belong.*" She read the preprinted words. "Do you all accept your choosing witch's dominion and agree to live by the witchworld rules?" Each of the thirteen warlocks said, "I do." The fourteenth glaringly missing. A few witches expressed concerns about his whereabouts and what'd happened to Zelda. Not one Helwig sat in the room, which meant no one would choose Joshua and the third warlock, unless by a Hail Mary from another coven.

"Each warlock will come to the podium in your pre-selected order. You know who is vying for you by the names on the sign-up sheet. Those witches will state their proposal in two minutes or less. You may ask questions, then make your choice all within two minutes. By now, you've spoken with each witch. The witches will provide a counteroffer within the allotted time, and you may change your mind." Sage paused to recall the rules for a situation she didn't think had ever occurred. "For warlocks selected by Zelda Helwig, you may decline the offer, or hold your decision until later. However, since she's not here, she forfeits her rights to you, and another witch is free to choose you. Or you're free to leave." She perused the eager young men. "Understood?" They all assented by nodding and otherwise verbalizing their affirmative responses. Joshua and the other warlock Zelda had chosen stood next to each other, arms crossed over their chests, seething in silence. Their brows furrowed in tandem.

Energized by the upcoming fun, witches whooped and clapped. Warlock numbers had dwindled over the last several years, and this solstice festival marked the largest group of unbonded warlocks they'd seen in years. The warlocks were not born to any modern witch, but possessed witch blood in their bloodlines. The growth in numbers alone was cause for celebration.

Sage called warlock number one. Stepping to her seat behind the podium, she tuned out the room. Her sight kept drifting to the closed door. One part wistful, the other part a slow-building resentment thawing the ice encasing her.

The process continued until Joshua's name hit the list. He approached the podium, and Sage joined him, standing closer than she wanted. He eased aside so as not to touch her. The heat of his anger sailed off him.

"Joshua. What do you want to do?" she asked. Despite what'd happened, he didn't fit in her coven. Half-assed magic and the thirty seconds of sex told her nothing about his potential. Sage feared whoever bonded him may travel a long road to train him. He had handsome and brawn going for him. Well, that and his large, but sorely lacking-in-talent tool. None of which were enough. Sage had the feeling he thought his enormous prick made up for his expertise. She hid a smile behind her hand.

"I'd like him to join my coven," Misty shouted, rising from her chair. "I have a young witch who needs a third warlock."

Shock zipped up Sage's spine. She didn't realize Misty's younger witches had multiple warlocks. Not unheard of, but junior witches had only one warlock unless they needed extra protection, especially with the recent dwindling warlock numbers.

"Do you want to join the Medeiros coven?" Sage asked Joshua. "Misty is the High Priestess of the large San Francisco Bay region. Very prestigious covens."

Before Joshua uttered a word, a commotion redirected attention to the main doors, both sides rolled wide open. Zelda and her entourage had arrived in the nick of time.

"I believe Joshua is mine," the older witch announced from the double doorway. Three warlocks flanked her. "If he so chooses, of course. Joshua, I stand by my promises. Promises I doubt being a third warlock to a mediocre witch could match."

With a huff, Misty sat down. "Fine. Whatever. He's all yours." She grinned at Sage, then texted her: *Don't really need him. Doing you a favor to get him out of your... hair.*

A dancing penis emoji in Misty's text forced Sage to stifle a fit of laughter. The laughter caught in her throat when Zelda and her three warlocks stepped inside the room. Rafael stood centered in the doorway alone.

Her heart stopped beating, then zoomed into fifth gear. The glimpse of him kick-started her desire, and joy jammed her hollows once again, except that freaky crater of missing magic.

His gaze swept the room, landed on her for a second and bounced onward. No recognition, no joy, nothing in his eyes. He strode forward and awkwardly linked his arm through Zelda's arm, as if responding to an unspoken command. Curious chaos set the room buzzing.

Gasping, Sage clamped onto the edges of the podium, using it to prop up her legs threatening to buckle and dump her on the plank floor. Ricky and Jessica rushed to her side, ready to catch her if she fell. They couldn't catch her heart from shattering into pieces and pinging her rib cage.

"Call the meeting to order," Jessica ordered.

Air lodged in Sage's throat. She'd shed her last tears over her parents' death and had not shed another since. In that moment, she wanted to smack Zelda upside the head and demand answers from Rafael. No tears, just recriminations and epic bewilderment.

"He doesn't belong to you now. Don't fight her over this," Jessica hissed. "She's not worth shirking your duties and new leadership role over. You trained for this all your life. Don't let one warlock destroy you."

"I know all that." Sage spoke through gritted teeth, her voice almost a growl. She banged her palm on the microphone several times to restore order to the room. "Settle down. Let's finish the lottery."

Everyone returned to their seats, making room for the Helwig entourage in the rear. Rafael sat next to a smirking Zelda. Sage caught his eye, and they locked gazes for a few too quick seconds. A spark of recognition widened his eyes for a fraction before Zelda leaned over to whisper in his ear. Sage looked away from all that was unholy.

"Joshua, since Zelda's here, do you accept her bid and the Helwig coven?"

He seemed to hem and haw a bit, his focus bouncing from Misty to Zelda, then landing on her. "Thought you'd make a bid for me. Guess your rep was overrated. I need an older witch who can teach me what you lack," he said in such a snide tone, Sage wanted to smack him to next Friday.

"Well, then, have at her." Sage waved her arm in Zelda's direction. "He's all yours, Zelda." She bit her tongue to halt the words she wanted to spew out, and to stop the same old litany vaulting to her mind about not having the right character, smarts, or dedication to follow in her mother's footsteps. An epic shitshow had ruined her day, and she wanted it done, wanted every non-Wilde witch and warlock to get the hell off her property.

With another nasty hiss, Jessica pried the microphone from Sage's grip. "It's settled. Joshua goes to Zelda Helwig." Her clap met half-hearted applause from the audience.

Joshua stomped to the Helwig coven, his features stormy dark. Zelda gestured to an empty chair next to her and he sat, squishing Zelda between himself and Rafael. She laid her hand proprietarily on both Joshua's and Rafael's thighs.

Sage wanted to upchuck the last three days and pretend they never existed. Sure as the fog promised to roll in over the bay tonight, the witchworld would see a new Sage, a new order, a new everything. She may have lost Rafael to the vilest witch in Oz, but she'd damn sure not lose the role defined by the Wilde High Priestesses who'd preceded her. Not now. Not ever.

Between burying her emotions and Jessica bolstering her up to manage the lottery, a grueling couple hours later, one last name remained on the list.

Despite her aunt's nagging, a renewed eagerness to plead her case for Rafael sent a thrill through her chest. Maybe he played Zelda by hanging with her since she'd brought him to the festival. Whatever.

She'd lure him from the hag for good.

"Last but not least, the final candidate is Rafael Reyes," Jessica called out. "Rafael, please advance and make your choice."

He remained fixed in place, his confusion clear as his eyes bore into Zelda. Excited chatter and murmuring rippled through the audience.

Sage leaned over the mic Jessica had returned to the podium. "Rafael, you must follow the process since two High Priestesses are vying for you."

"I don't understand," he said loud enough for the entire room to overhear.

Why is he hanging all over Zelda as if she's the only steak at a tofu convention? Sage wanted to fly to him, extract him from the Helwig realm, and shake sense into him.

"Oh, dear boy. Yes, let's play this out." Zelda blew out an exaggerated sigh. "Go and hear what High Priestess Wilde has to say. I'm curious what the twit will spew myself." She tapped Rafael's thigh. He wiped his palms on his jeans and walked toward the podium.

Burying her annoyance at Zelda's weary insults, Sage's senses feasted on him. She recalled the touch of his fingers, the warmth of his body, the firm softness of his lips. He wore the same gray T-shirt and jeans from earlier that morning, but Sage noticed a pendant hanging off his neck and a beaded bracelet he hadn't worn when he'd left her room earlier. As he walked closer, Sage identified the silver pendant. Perspiration formed on her chest, and she wanted to wither and die. The bobcat necklace meant he belonged to Zelda, or at the very least promised to choose her, after already accepting her bid, plea, or blackmail, however Zelda couched it.

A grievous loss tried to submerge Sage, and she rammed the grief below her rising aether. The telltale headache flirted behind her eyes. Grit hadn't reached her eyeballs, but one more misstep, threat, or horrendous news byte might trigger a swell.

When Rafael tipped his head back, not one iota of recognition flickered in his blank stare. Flustered beyond reason, she buried her emotions so deep, she'd need three earth witches to dig them out. Everything felt out of whack. What new clusterfuck had Zelda caused? Sage needed to prevent the Helwigs from plowing over the western region.

No time like the present.

Everything changed, and her future solidified in her mind. No more raver. No more agreeing to the Helwigs and their kind or taking bullshit from the witches of the West. They'd voted her in, and she'd be the High Priestess they needed, whether they wanted her or not.

She slammed her palm on the microphone. "I'm taking fifteen minutes for a private chat with Rafael before I make my offer. Since he's the last unbonded warlock on the list, you are all free to leave, except for Zelda."

Enthralled, not one person moved nor objected. Perfect fodder to end the festival. One reason they did a warlock lottery, for fun and entertainment. *Where's the hot-buttered popcorn when you needed it?* Sage felt far from entertained.

"Time for talk is over. Make your bid and be done," Zelda announced. Her beaming smile could have charmed the most venomous of snakes. Sage noticed a nervousness in Zelda as she rolled and unrolled the cuffs of her long sleeves, distracting her hands or her magic. Who knew?

"As regional High Priestess, it's my right to talk to any warlock during the lottery. Check the bylaws," Sage said. "Meanwhile, Rafael and I will talk on the rear patio. I'll be done when I'm done."

"That's bullshit," Zelda screeched, springing out of her seat. Her witches and warlocks closed ranks around her. "There's no such bylaw granting the regional High Priestess extra rights."

"*Au contraire.* Read the fucking bylaws," Sage shouted, confident in her memory of witchworld rules. Witches across the room scrambled to engage their tablets and phones. Even if it wasn't an obscure rule, Zelda could suck it up and die for all she cared.

She clenched Rafael's hand, and a strangely familiar herbal scent wafted off the wooden beads on his charm bracelet. Their touch incited a dance of opposing magic, not the magic of their connection, but Helwig magic meeting Sage's magic. Zelda's witch-air, untapped and unknown to Rafael, but ready for commands.

Zelda had already bonded him. The bonding explained the new void inside her. *Holy shit on a broken broomstick.*

Aether sand coated her eyeballs, and she felt her irises change to a deeper emerald on their way to obsidian. His untapped magic, whether Zelda's or whatever else he possessed deep in his core, whipped her aether inside her, like the branches on the evergreens dancing to gusts of wind.

Sweat dampened Rafael's warm fingers, but he didn't withdraw his hand as she led him out the back. Shouts and commotion accompanied the slam of the door as Sage shut out the chaos.

Not caring whether her demon eyes frightened him, she dropped his hand and spun on him. "Did she bond you?"

His face was a mix of fear and dread, but he didn't move away. He slipped his fists in his front pockets as if to stop them from touching her. "Guess so. She did a ritual and I accepted. She said I'm her warlock now. I feel her magic inside me. Don't know how to work it yet."

"Why? What's going on?" Sage stamped her foot on the pavers, trying to tamp down her rising aether as well.

"What do you mean? She discovered me. I made promises to her." Unease flitted across his face. He planted a foot of distance between them. "I mean one of her warlocks, Sammy, discovered me."

A breeze blew the scent of the wooden beads up to her nostrils again. Sage crinkled her nose. She wracked her brain to place the herb. Zelda had spelled Rafael, but she didn't want to touch the bracelet until she recognized the scent. Didn't want to cause potential further damage by removing it. The spell affected his memory, made him lethargic with a skewed sense of reality. She tested her theory.

"Don't you remember *us*?" She burned with a desire to touch him, but curled her fists at her sides, her fingernails biting into her skin. "The night we spent talking, planning. Kissing, touching, and wanting so much more." Urgency caused her pitch to escalate as her eyes began to normalize.

Rafael squinted and his lips pinched in a grim line. "I remember seeing you a couple days ago from afar. We've never talked. I think I'd remember kissing you." No grin, only somberness as if resolved to his fate.

Thuds hit the door from inside the witch-house. Sage heard Ricky shouting, barring the door. Probably the Helwigs trying to reach Sage and blast her a new ass. She tuned out the ruckus.

Rafael spun on his heels toward the door. Another whiff from the beads hit her and crashed through the doors of her memories. Datura or maybe henbane carrying a belladonna—deadly nightshade—kick. Enough to suppress his memory by slowing down his metabolism and brain function, with a sleepy, hallucinogenic affect.

Sage lunged forward and ripped the leather band off Rafael's wrist. She flung the bracelet in an empty plant pot, needing to preserve it for evidence.

"Hey!" Rafael yelped, rubbing his wrist.

"Sorry, it's spelled. Come closer." She gestured him closer, but he backstepped. "Please. I can fix this."

"Fix what?" He scratched his head. "Sage, right?"

"Yes, I'm Sage." Relief skated across her shoulders. But he would not return to normal fast enough without magical intervention. "I can heal your confusion."

"Okay," he said haltingly. "What—"

As she touched her fingertips to his forehead, something banged the door again. Quickly, she whispered a counter-spell to dispel the effects of the charmed beads. Might not be fast enough, but it would break the spell Zelda had plonked on the beads. She uttered, "So mote it be," aloud and smoothed her fingertips over the lines etched on his brow.

Pain arced across Rafael's pale face. "What did you do?" He rubbed his forehead, pressed his palm over his heart, then over his abdomen. "I don't feel so hot."

Sage waved her open hands and pushed fresh witch-air at his nose, trying to rid his senses of the stench from Zelda's charm bracelet. "Inhale deeply, then exhale," she said. "Again and again!"

"Sage?" Puppet strings seemed to jerk his head up, and he glanced around the patio, at the door holding back the chaos unfurling on the other side. "What's going on?"

"Do you remember me? When did we meet?"

"Yeah. We met yesterday."

Sage clutched the bobcat pendant in her fist. "Do you remember Zelda Helwig giving this to you?"

He tipped his chin down. "Nope."

"Do you remember we spent the night together last night?" Silence gave his answer. "What do you recall?"

He slumped his butt atop the old, weathered picnic table, pain lancing his body, evidenced by the shudders renting him. "What's happening to me?"

"Zelda spelled you and used spelled charms to bury your memories and keep you compliant to her demands."

His spine jolted straight. "Spelled me how?"

"She coerced you, repressed your memories, suppressed your actions."

"Why?" He smoothed his fingers over his scalp, winced. "I'm roasting inside."

Sage mumbled another spell and sprinkled witch-water on him, expanded her witch-air spell to cool him off. "The pain you're feeling is from Zelda bonding you without your permission. She coerced your actions."

Nobody had busted the door down, and someone must have barricaded the main entrance to the witch-house, otherwise, witches and warlocks would've swarmed the patio. The break wouldn't last forever. Laying her hand over his heart, Sage intoned another counter-spell, hoping to scrub out the coercion spell quicker. "Do you remember anything?"

"Warlocks abducted me. Told me it was a hazing

ritual. You said nothing about hazing, so I didn't believe them."

Relief untied another knot in Sage's shoulders. "They lied to you. What else?"

"They locked me in a room on the Helwig covenstead. Then Zelda came in and asked if I'd accept her bond. She made me recite..." His voice trailed off.

"That bitch." Shock seized him with a sudden jerk of his head and a wide-eyed expression. "Sage," he breathed out her name, all the weight of their intense time together in the one word. "It's coming back."

Sage leaned down and pressed her lips to his. Instinctively, he stood and wrapped her in his weak arms as if she belonged there, the only one who could re-energize him. He deepened the kiss until they were both forced to seek air. She mashed her breasts against his chest, feeling the rapid beat of his heart. He buried his face in her hair, his hands smoothing over her butt and up her back. His touch intoxicated her more than any tequila shot.

"Do you recall us now?" she asked, emotion splintering her voice.

"She erased you from my memories. I remember now."

Sage sagged against him. "How bad is the pain?"

"Lava's gushing through me." He sifted his hand through her hair. "Sage, god, you're the sunshine in my dark hell."

"Do you still want me?" she demanded, loving his hand plying her hair.

"More than anything I've ever wanted."

"Good. Because I refuse to give you up to Zelda. I need you, want you. The goddess meant for you to come to this festival. For us. You're the only thing that matters."

His mouth opened but nothing came out. He scratched his cheek and said, "Not sure I can join your world. It's already done a number on me. But I want you more than anything I've ever wanted in my life."

"Do you trust me?"

"Absolutely. Can't we just run away together?" He quirked a sluggish eyebrow.

"Everything will improve once we sort out this bonding business. If Zelda doesn't release you without a fight, I'll compel her to break the bond. She forced an illegal coercion spell on you, not giving you the choice you're allowed. She'll face extreme consequences either way."

"Then what happens?" Wincing, he rubbed his stomach.

"Then I bond you. If you'll accept me." She winked.

Footsteps rushed around the corner of the witch-house. The clock had run out.

"Sage!" Her aunt halted on the walkway at the side of the building. "You need to bring the meeting to order. The Helwigs are out of control. They're gunning for you." Jessica's tabby familiar raced around the patio searching for threats against its master. The cat stopped and growled at the door where the internal uproar played out. Sage tipped her head to the side, a memory attempting to disrupt her. She thrust it into a crypt for another time.

"Go settle them down," Sage commanded. "We're coming. Also, pull the bylaws. Zelda committed an illegal coercion spell on Rafael. *After* abducting him."

Jessica's jaw dropped, but a small smile played at the corners of her lips, and she sprinted away.

"Don't go." Rafael dug his hands in her hair, his grip pulling her head closer. His lips landed on hers possessively, tempting, and oh so evocative that Sage felt like drowning in him. "I remember this. Kissing you. You're like a drug. My salvation."

"Then don't stop kissing me." She once again parted her lips to deepen the exquisite kiss.

He tangoed his tongue around hers. No one had ever kissed Sage the way Rafael kissed her, like he'd chosen her from a stadium packed with all the women in the world. Like she was his air, his heart, and soul.

So absorbed in Rafael's masterful kiss, Sage didn't hear the door burst open.

"Hands off my warlock, you slut!" A blast of wind preceded Zelda onto the patio, a squall shoving Sage and Rafael apart.

Chapter 12

Zelda's witch-air howled and gusted against Sage. Each time Rafael reached for her, the tempest blasted Sage farther across the patio until she landed at the perimeter of the woods. Sage's own magic kicked in and prevented her from crashing to the ground. A ring of blue fire encapsulated her, and she tossed out fire-tinged air magic to deflect Zelda's magic.

Rafael remembered Sage telling him a secret that she held all natural magical elements, a rarity among the witchworld. Then why had he accepted Zelda's offer? Why wouldn't he want to join forces with a more powerful witch? One as beautiful, smart, and sexy as Sage. One who he'd connected with on a more emotional and visceral level than magic. The memories of their night together emerged from the shallow grave unearthed in his mind. Rage smothered the memories to concentrate on his current predicament. His fury at Zelda for treating him like a possession, stealing his freedom, and for her betrayal of Sage howled inside him.

The tug on his derived witch-air from Zelda brought him closer to her. He fought the compulsion to keep his distance. But she called the shots, and he had no magical leg to stand on considering his untrained abilities.

Witches and warlocks surrounded them on the patio, attempting to stop Zelda or trying to aid her, depending on which side of the sandbox they played in. Magic whipped the air in tangible air ropes. Leafy vines and lightning bolts tried to slice through Zelda's solid walls of air separating him and her from the rest of the world.

A booming voice cut through the chaos, and he drilled through the foggy air to see Jessica Wilde standing on the picnic table, a megaphone hiding her face.

"Stop this at once. Stand down," she bellowed.

It took a few more commands before the magic simmered. The jittery, tense crowd lingered in groups around the patio's perimeter. A light wind of air magic ruffled hair and clothing. The lightning bolts fizzled, and the thick vines retreated into the ground. Familiars leaped, flew, and scurried to their witches. Sage's owl familiar soared above their heads, dragging glowing ropes of magic in its feet and beak. A fluffy gray and brown tabby squatted on guard at Jessica's feet, hissing and yowling at anyone attempting to approach her except for Wilde coven members.

Sage charged toward him from the woods where the wind had caged her. He liquified at her fierce beauty, her hair swirling in tangles around her head. Panting and vibrating with emotions, she came abreast of him. He picked leaves out of her hair and brushed dirt off her arm, then took her hand in his.

The moment he touched her, a strange magic inside her linked to that deep untapped well inside him that not even Zelda's magic touched.

The fire searing his insides erupted anew, and the pain of Zelda's illegal acts killed any other sensation. He dropped Sage's hand and clutched his arms over his chest, needing to staunch the pain. He swallowed bile, looked for an escape route before he made a fool of himself.

"What in the goddess's name, Zelda?" Sage yelled. "You bonded Rafael without his permission. A major-ass infraction." Gasps broke the silence, but Sage continued, undeterred by their hundred or so witnesses. "I demand that you break your bond now or you'll suffer the fullest extent of the witchworld law."

"Tack on illegal magic raising and a boatload of other charges," Jessica spat out. "What were you thinking, Zelda? Not only did you break the warlock lottery rules by not giving Rafael a choice, but you bonded him without his permission? Who does that?"

"*How* did she do it, is what I want to know?" Another High Priestess stepped to Sage's other side. "Well, speak up, witch. What do you have to say for yourself?"

Zelda finger-brushed her snarled hair and smoothed down her skewed blouse. A small bobcat familiar leaped off her upper arm, crouched at her feet, and glared at Jessica's tabby. "I did nothing of the kind. Mr. Reyes and I reached an understanding earlier. If you read the bylaws regarding the warlock lottery, you'll find a clause that allows a warlock to choose a High Priestess without going through the lottery if he finds the perfect fit." She folded the long sleeves of her tunic up, then down, something Rafael had seen her sister do. She did another fold, then down and he realized it was a sign. Imelda Helwig nodded at her sister.

All eyes shifted to Rafael. The blood rushed down his face, and he sucked in fresh air before he crashed. "Zelda's warlocks abducted me and locked me in a room at her covenstead. She spelled me. Next thing I know, I'm here. Sage broke the spell and released my memories."

Zelda's inky eyebrows arched. "How did I spell you, Rafael?"

He scratched his head. "How the fuck do I know? I'm not a witch."

"You used a coercion spell on him, a mix of henbane, datura, and belladonna." Sage gauged the shocked reactions of the witches. "I tore a charmed bracelet off Rafael that kept the spell alive. She smothered his memories so he wouldn't remember he had chosen me."

A tiny smile curled the corners of Zelda's mouth. "Find the charm. Prove these accusations you're slinging." A handful of witches and warlocks began combing the wind-blown patio and nearby woods.

Fiery pain lanced Rafael in two. "Sage," he whispered. "I don't feel so hot."

She touched his arm, a soothing press of her fingers. "He's fighting her magic. Isn't that proof enough of a coerced bond?" Sage took his hand in hers, her slender fingers soft and inviting. He never wanted to let her go again. "Let's sit inside," she suggested. "Don't fight it." She addressed the nearest witch. "Where's Aspen? I need a potion to soothe his pain."

"I can remove his pain," Zelda tossed in. "He's suffering the usual new-bonded-warlock affects."

"Does that lie keep you warm at night?" Sage

rebutted, and Rafael knew how much he was out of his depths. Holding Sage's hand offered him the impetus to stay and learn about his new world... as long as she stood by his side.

A Helwig warlock stepped between Zelda and Rafael, one of the ones who'd kidnapped him. With all his lagging strength, Rafael hauled back his arm and slugged the warlock so hard and fast the warlock didn't have time to raise magic before he slumped to the ground, out like a light. "That's for kidnapping me, asshole." He shoved his fist against Zelda's upper arm. He didn't give a rat's ass that she was a woman. "Kill the bond, or so help me god, I will bury you."

A Wilde warlock rushed to Sage, dangling the bracelet. Sage sniffed it, frowned.

"What's wrong?" Rafael asked.

"It's dead." Zelda grinned at Sage's proclamation. "Her air magic rendered it void." Sage tossed the bracelet on the ground. "Undo the bond. Rafael chooses me."

"Where's your proof?" Zelda palmed her moonstone ring as if gaining power from it. "I will not undo the bond. You're overstepping your boundaries, Sage Wilde." She held her hand out to Rafael, and he retreated a step. "You chose me. Come. You're mine. I will not release you to this stupid child."

More anger than he'd ever experienced thrashed through him again. He didn't know a way out, other than to let Sage duke it out for him. Otherwise, he'd be stuck bound to this old hag until when? Until she died? Until he died? *Two hundred bucks for a clue, Alex.*

Sage shivered, flexed her hand in his, and he let go, flinging off the magic she emitted. An intangible roiling mass of fire, loamy air, a drizzle of water and vines growing out of the ground and snaking over the patio alarmed the crowd into backing away from Sage. Her eyes turned dark as night, surrounded by a glimmering silver halo. Shimmery bands of white magic whipped and swirled around her, the electricity crackling in the air.

"Do you trust me?" she asked, her breath warm against his ear.

Without a doubt, he nodded. He had found his home in her, and he'd cherish her with every fiber of his being... and fight to the death for her.

"What do you want, Rafael? Who do you want to bond." Outside sounds dropped to nothing, unable to compete with the dynamic hum of Sage's magic.

He lifted his head, raised his voice for the crowd ogling the train wreck on the patio. "I never chose Zelda Helwig. I demand she release whatever fucked-up bond and spells she dumped on me. I choose the light, the sunshine, the magic, the home I found among the Wilde coven. I choose Sage Wilde." His bold stare shot switchblades at Zelda. *If only.* "Release me now or I will destroy you." He ripped the chain off his neck and flung the pendant where it clinked to the pavers at Zelda's feet.

Two more wild cats sprang off her and surrounded her feet, growling and snarling. His own bobcat tattoo—not that he'd accepted it—remained static on his arm.

"Big words from an untrained warlock." A glower flitted across her features. "I can asphyxiate you in two seconds. Or do you prefer to die in an inferno?"

"You heard him. Release him. Now." Sage advanced a step toward Zelda. A bobcat screeched at her, forcing her to freeze. Rafael stretched out his arm to hold her back, as if to protect her.

A cacophony of loud gasps echoed through the crowd. Zelda jerked back from Sage, clutching her neck, her features screwed up in horror. Rafael checked Sage from his peripheral vision. The black and silver of her eyes, the tangible aural glowing bands drifting and seething around her scared the life out of him. And everyone else by the alarm on their faces and the distance they put between themselves and Sage.

Wind funnels stirred up a symphony of sound as they whipped the tree branches around them. Evergreen needles gyrated in the air. Rain coalesced into a typhoon, dripping from a clear blue sky. Tiny stars tumbled from the sky, trickling within the wind and water. Embers and ashes fell upon the Helwigs and their supporters, their magic ineffectual against the stars singeing their clothing. Sage circled her hand and drew a blue fire ring around the patio, preventing escape or containing the magic. Didn't matter.

Zelda twirled her arms above her head, stirring up a wind storm. It plucked on Rafael's center of magic. He needed an outlet to rid his body of her, but he didn't know how yet.

"Drop the magic, Sage," Zelda screeched.

"Break the bond," she replied, calm radiating off her despite the magical chaos. "He chose me."

"I will not. I invoked my right to bond him. A fight over a warlock during a lottery means the warlock walks away. He can't choose or bond any witch from our region for three years. Read the bylaws." She threw Sage's words back at her.

Was it true? Rafael's racing heart stuttered.

A band of air whacked Rafael across the face, smothering him, muffling him above all. The bands spiraled around him, cementing him to the pavers. His thoughts remained clear, and he could still see and talk. The magic inside him remained. He fought the witch-air, knowing he couldn't use magic against Zelda. The bond prevented him from doing so. But something inside him disputed that notion, and he worked on internalizing his thoughts to match his magical action and reaction.

"Screw you, Zelda. You broke the rules when you magically raped him." Lightning bolts erupted over Zelda's head, threatening, but not harming. Yet. Sage's owl familiar directed the bolts in a ring of fire surrounding the Helwig coven members.

Zelda signaled Imelda and several witches from her coven, and they broke apart the fire ring, blasting wind, water, and their own fire through it. Another signal and they hurled a combined fiery ball, propelled by witch-air, at Sage.

Sage thwarted the attack, but the effort strained her. Perspiration formed on her upper lip, and her cheeks blazed crimson. Her magic thrust Zelda's entire coven and her allies to the edge of the woods.

The threats to Sage drove Rafael's every command into the magic inside him, battling against Zelda's influence. He cracked his knuckles, the sound loud against the swirling and popping magic. "How dare you threaten my witch, you fucking bitch?" He chucked fire-tinged air at Zelda, catching her off guard, giving her no chance of a counterattack. How was he able to use magic against Zelda? The fire and air felt eerily similar to the magic Sage wielded.

As Sage had threatened, figurative flying monkeys and ninja fairies broke out to fight Zelda's ineffectual air magic. Rafael stood, arms outstretched, immune to any magic. Another few seconds flew by that seemed like hours, air against air, fire against fire, intangible but powerful. After one last thrust of rebound magic at Zelda, her hands scratched at her neck, her mouth hung open in horror, and she crumpled to the ground in a heap of billowing black clothing. Her bobcat familiars clambered onto her body and morphed into their tattoo forms beneath her clothing. The bobcat that'd so far remained dormant on Rafael's arm, slithered off his skin in earth-tone shades of ink. The ink blotches slinked to Zelda's body where she reabsorbed them on her right hand.

Magic faded, and the air stilled. Zelda gasped out several gusts of air and sparks dripped off her fingers, splatting onto the pavers. That foreign entity inside Rafael disintegrated into dust and rushed out of him, alleviating the pain he'd felt since Sage broke Zelda's spells. The fire eating him alive tempered and dulled. He'd decimated his connection to Zelda. Again, how the hell had he managed it?

Imelda rushed to her sister's prone body and squatted on the ground. Her fingers searched for a pulse until she stood, spine rigid and glowered at Rafael. "You've killed her." Not one tear filled her eyes.

Seething, Sage stood next to Rafael, smelling of burnt sage and brimstone. Crackling, stinging magic wafted off her and mingled within the residual magic. He'd take it any day over Zelda's toxic magic.

"No. She killed herself," Sage said. "A warlock is incapable of using magic against his bonded witch. She brought this on herself by defying the witchworld laws."

Jessica approached Imelda, Ben in tow behind her. "I'm sorry for your loss, Imelda. Zelda has always been a loose cannon, and her number came up. Now take her body and all your people and please go."

Imelda's glare at Sage threatened to kill. "You will rue this day. With *you* at the helm of the western region, you'll destroy us all." She addressed the crowd at large. "You all made the biggest mistake of your lives."

Chapter 13

Sage rushed a silent and skittish Rafael to her bedroom, the safest place on the compound. Ricky followed and remained on guard in the hallway. She shut her bedroom door, locked it, and faced Rafael. "We'll be safe here. My witches and warlocks will kill the chaos." As much as she wanted to wilt to her knees in exhaustion and magic depletion, she needed to ensure Rafael was okay. "Did you feel the bond break? Like a knife slicing through an intestine."

Pasty and sweaty, he nodded, balled his hands at his sides. "What did I do? How is she dead?"

Sage gloved his left fist in her hands and coaxed him closer. He didn't resist. "You did nothing. She caused her own magic to lose control when it reacted to the magic she granted you." Sage paused, wondering if Zelda's magic also reacted aversely to her aether. She'd never seen the like, although she'd heard of witch-air smothering a person. "The witch-air stole the air from her lungs, deflating them. It smothered her. She brought this on herself." Sage wasn't a hundred percent convinced her aether didn't play a part, and she knew she had to get it under complete control before her world crumbled around her.

"I still feel weird." He recoiled.

"It'll take time for the magic to dispel." Sage tried to wrap her arms around him, but too much distance separated them. She dropped his hand, leaving her frigid, despite the fire roaring through her body. Magic refilled the crater inside her, a return to her new normal of rising aether and Rafael's strange brew.

"Part of it's normal," he confessed, dipping his head to study his feet.

"I know." Did she? He felt more magic than an unbonded warlock should. But she let it go. No sense in freaking him out all over again. "You're reacting to all the magic on the compound. Everyone will suffer until my aether disburses." She snorted, trying to diffuse the awkwardness. "I promise you'll feel better."

Tension fled Rafael's body by the drooping of his taut shoulders. He took a cautious step forward and plucked a vine from her tangled hair. "You've got vines in your hair." He tried to pull another twig from her damp hair, and she winced from the sting on her scalp. "Sorry. Won't come out. Damn, it's like it's... growing out of your head." He chuckled, fighting his shock.

Smiling to set him at ease, she clasped his hand again. "It'll die and fall out."

Horror masked his face. Until the unthinkable happened and the mask slipped. He busted out in laughter so infectious they both sank to the floor, rolling and clutching their stomachs.

"Laughter's killer medicine to recover from a shitshow," she said between bouts of giggles.

"God, I hope so."

"I promise you we'll laugh a lot." She rolled closer to him and they both lay on their sides facing each other on the dense wool rug. She inhaled the welcome scent of him.

"What about romance? And sex?" He cradled her face in his hands, his touch gentle and loving.

Feeling the depth of their connection, she gazed deeply into the warmth of his eyes. His tender and affectionate touch conveyed his desire and devotion. As he leaned in to kiss her, time stood still. His lips met hers with a longing that had been building for what felt like an eternity. The kiss was soft and slow, yet filled with an intense passion that took her breath away.

She savored the salty taste of his lips and the warmth of his body as they held each other in a tight embrace. The world around them faded away, leaving only the two of them lost in each other. As the kiss ended, he pulled back slightly with a soft smile and sparkling eyes.

"I can promise tons of romance," she said, and twined her arms around his neck. The strength in his firm body pressed against hers and just his mere presence provided an anecdote to a disastrous day. "I can definitely promise lots of sex."

"Ditto." Easing back, he let out a frustrated groan. "Not yet. Not like this."

Sage fake-pouted. "I know."

"You need to bond me now. You need my protection more than ever. That Imelda bitch is gonna seek revenge."

Joy overcame her, and her limbs melted onto the

rug. Stars sprayed the air above their heads and rained down in rose petals all over them.

Rafael caught red petals on his palm and inhaled them. "Is that a yes?"

"Absolutely. Everything I offered stands. But we can't until Z's magic is out of your system."

His shoulders sagged, and the rose petals fluttered from his hands. "How long?"

"A week maybe." Before he reacted, she pressed her mouth to his again, and they kissed until her head stopped spinning, and a knock on the door interrupted them. She wiped a smudge of ash off his temple. "Take a shower. Rinse that hag off your skin. I need to end the festival. I'll ward the room, and no one will bug you."

"Sage," he breathed out her name in the way she loved. "I think I'm gonna love it here. Or wherever *you* are." He pushed up off the floor and helped her stand, his hand warm and strong gloved around hers.

"Well, good. I feel the same about you." Without an ounce of remorse or regret, she watched him saunter into her bathroom and close himself inside.

Sage unlocked and opened the door, and Jessica's tabby, Pebbles, darted in ahead of Jessica. The cat growled and hissed at the bathroom door.

Sage rounded on her aunt, resigned. Also confused and ticked. "It was you in the woods threatening me yesterday morning." No question, just plain fact.

The door shut, and Ben and Ricky's voices drifted away. Jessica looked her point-blank in the eyes. "How'd you figure it out?"

"Pebbles. I recognized her growl and hiss." Irritation flared in her chest. "Who did your dirty work since you were at the house? Why would you all threaten me?"

"Ben and your cousins helped." Jessica wrung her hands. "I wanted you to treat the scare as a threat from your enemies, from the Helwigs. To get angry, to show every witch in the region that you won't take crap from anyone. You need to stop the partying, grow up and take the reins, accept your heritage."

"It was *your* heritage," Sage reminded Jessica, not unkindly.

"The role was never mine. You're more powerful. Younger, more progressive, focused, and aware. More educated. With your aether, you can rule the witchworld someday. Your mother prophesied it after she conceived you."

Sage's eyelids fluttered, and shock beat down her anger. "You and Mom planned this?"

"Of course. That's why she trained you for this role. Unfortunately, it landed in your lap too soon." Jessica squeezed Sage's hand. "I will always be here for you. I'll be your second, but we'll also need to train your sisters and cousins to run the coven and region."

"Yeah. After today's crap-storm, I could've bitten the bullet and left you all high and dry."

"Well, you showed the California region your strength going against a Helwig. Rumor in the entire region is that they made the right choice in choosing you."

"Did you doubt it?" Relief streamed through Sage's limbs.

"Not for a second. But you'd marched down a path that could've changed everyone's opinions. At least tell me you have a new warlock now." Jessica's focus drifted to the bathroom door, the sound of the shower white noise to mask the occasional sound from outside.

"I do, and more." Warmth swamped Sage, and she

was dying to join Rafael in the shower. Alas, duty prevailed.

"Don't fall in love yet. You can't let love blind you to growing the coven and proving our strength. If you fail, we may never rule the region again. You have plenty of time and the grit to enforce change, to gain respect. Maybe not the Helwigs' respect and allegiance, but more than enough to keep your majority."

"Too late. I'm falling." The water shut off. The shower door clicked open and shut.

"He ignites you." Jessica's features softened. "Oh, honey. I'm happy for you. Promise you won't let him interfere with your duties."

"He's the strongest warlock I've ever seen. I need him. Now more than ever. Together, we'll kill it. Mark my words." Sage knew the moment she'd met Rafael they'd make a formidable pair in the witchworld. She'd show every witch on Earth how her gut never let her down. And she'd prove it while falling in love with him. Rafael at her side gave her a sense of reassurance, and she felt unstoppable. *Party girl will not define me ever again. So mote it be!*

☪☪☪

The door to Sage's office burst open and Rafael rushed through. "Sorry, babe. I finished an installation job early and came to work on the cabin. Lost track of time."

Grinning, Sage shut her laptop and relaxed back against her desk chair. Ten days after the Summer Solstice festival, they'd fallen into a beautiful and happy pattern. Although Rafael worked and lived in town, his time there neared a close. Every moment with him was better than the last and she didn't see it changing soon, or ever. And she wanted him on the covenstead.

Although she'd never know if her aether magic played a part in Zelda's death, every witness at the catastrophe concluded that the witch's death was accidental, brought upon by Zelda's illegal and unnatural bonding of Rafael and her magic reacting adversely. Sage had to take the consensus at face value and start her new chapter ruling the region with Rafael. The western witchworld counted on her... and counted on her bonding Rafael to form the power duo she'd promised.

She slid an envelope across the desk. "Your first paycheck."

He slivered his eyes. "Huh?"

"We pay our warlocks. We don't expect you to quit your jobs and work for free, especially in a more dangerous job."

Rafael didn't touch the envelope. "You're paying me to spend time with you? No, thanks. It's my honor to be your warlock... and your boyfriend."

"No, it's my honor to be your witch and girlfriend." Sage slid her chair back from the desk. "It's not a payoff. If your boss cuts your salary because of your warlock duties, we need to cover the difference. Honor doesn't pay your bills."

"How do you afford the pay? *You* don't work."

Sage's laughter echoed through the room. She didn't feel the least bit insulted. They hadn't much discussed the business side of managing the coven in their time together. Too much kissing and touching, laughing and learning about each other, and hiking in the woods. "My father was a high-profile attorney and a kick-ass investor, like his father. We hold active investments, which I might add, is at least a part-time job." She quirked her eyebrows. "Plus, every witch contributes in various cottage industries. Heck, my cousin Eden's a successful novelist."

Rafael sidled around the desk, and Sage rose to meet him in a passionate, soul-filled kiss. After they broke apart, she leaned her cheek against his chest, loving the scent and feel of him, from the fresh shampoo of his damp hair to his natural musk and the clean laundry fragrance of his dove-gray T-shirt.

"I want to contribute." He rested his chin on her head.

"Rafael, you already are contributing."

"Once you bond me, I'll need to be here full-time, which means I need to quit my job."

"Right," she said, her spine tensing.

"My boss has talked up selling his security firm in a year or two. He wants to train me on the business end, and he's giving me first dibs on buying the biz. He'll let me pay him in installments. Put my pay toward that." He squeezed her closer. "It's everything I've always wanted. Well, except for you." He nuzzled her neck and kissed the skin behind her ear, leaving goosebumps traveling down her neck.

Joy streamed through Sage, warm and comforting. She drew back and took his hand in hers. "I want to show you something."

"Then I've got a surprise for you." He followed her out of her office to a door across the hall.

Slow and hesitant, Sage opened the door to a smaller office, cleaned out except for an empty desk, bare shelves, and office equipment. "My father's office and man cave." The perfect office for Rafael to sit in front of the large window and watch the sunrise from inside the house. "It's your office now as my First

Warlock."

Rafael held a breath for the longest time before he exhaled. "Did you just say First Warlock?" He spun toward her, his mouth gaping.

She'd waited five extra days to ensure Zelda's magic had taken a hike. She didn't want any other magic interfering during the bonding ritual. They'd already planned for the ceremony that night. "Do you think you can run a security firm from here? You deserve all the conveniences of my home, my covenstead, our witchworld. This is your home too."

He trailed kisses from her jaw to her ear. "Already feels like home."

"Is that a yes?" His thumb traveled to first one nipple, then the other, rubbing them into stiff points, spiraling lust downward, and she gasped at the depths of her feelings.

"Oh, yeah." His lips rested on hers, and she drank him in until they parted, breathless as always when they kissed. "Follow me."

They strode out to the backyard. Through the trees, Sage spied fairy lights lighting up the marble gazebo her parents had built. Delight rippled in her chest. Her favorite place when she craved serenity. Candles lit the inside from the round table in the middle to the three marble benches inside the perimeter and on the two steps outside. A bottle of wine sat on the table next to plates of finger foods, the same food they'd eaten the fateful festival night.

Giggling, she spun in a circle. "This is enchanting. You did this?"

"It's why I ran late. Aspen helped." Apprehension smoothed out his grin.

Sage reached for his hand, squeezed and dropped it. "It won't hurt. Not like what Zelda did to you."

They'd already decided that sex was off the table for a while. They wanted to go slow and build their relationship without adding sex to the menu until they were ready. Sage didn't need the sex to understand his magic strength or to know his warlock powers matched her magic. She didn't need sex to strengthen an already perfect bond. Most of all, Sage didn't want to treat him like the myriad other warlocks she'd tested in bed. Rafael was too unique, and they had a lifetime to create their own special magic, in and outside the bedroom.

She picked up an unlit candle and lit the wick with her pointer finger. "Rafael Reyes, do you accept my bond of witch to warlock of your own free will?"

"I accept any way you want to bond me."

"Goddess, you heard his assent." Sage added other questions just in case. "Am I, Sage Wilde, or any other person or thing, coercing you, Rafael Reyes, to accept my bond?"

"Hell to the no." He vigorously shook his head.

"Goddess, you heard his answer." Sage lit another candle on the table, another point on the compass to signify his answer.

"Do you, Rafael Reyes, accept the witchworld rules?"

"Yes." Another lit candle.

Oh beautiful moon
Oh brilliant fire, which I hold in my hand
By the air that I breathe, by the breath within me
To Rafael Reyes, bound together I wish to be
I give you the magic of my body, my heart, my soul
Eternal and steadfast
I open my body to your magic
Call upon my magic as if it were your own

I'll never use my magic or yours against you
I will guard your powers as I guard my own
Link us together
Take this spell and make it be
As I will, so mote it be.

Rafael uttered the words Sage had him memorize. Once he repeated "so mote it be," they both blew out the candle in her hand.

Magic connected them, whipping inside her, and he bucked against her. She caught him in her arms, the candle tumbling to the marble floor. Awe spread across his face, the fairy lights reflecting diamonds in his eyes. Stars rose above their heads, twinkling brighter than the light strands.

Rafael's acceptance of her magic was nothing she'd ever experienced with any other warlock. Like his magic completed her. It seemed to strengthen her magic. Or maybe because she'd never fallen for a man like Rafael, her magic was purer and more tolerant.

"What do you feel?" Arms held above her head, she spun around the gazebo, directing the stars shooting from her fingers to the domed roof.

"Like my insides want to explode outside my body, and I'm the ignition for an inferno."

"Oh, no. It's not supposed to hurt." Dismayed, Sage dropped her arms and pulled her phone out of her back pocket. "I'll call Aspen for a pain potion."

He covered her fingers on her phone. "No. It's incredible. The magic's wanting to explode. It's me wanting to use your magic. Totally insane."

Sage leaned into him, and he embraced her, her body liquifying into his. "Thank the goddess." She vowed never to bring another warlock to the gazebo. It would always remain their sacred place.

"I feel alive for the first time in my life. All because of you." He tilted her head back, cupped her cheeks, and brought his mouth to hers. They kissed, their lips leisurely and tenderly exploring one another. When they parted, she felt her heart racing with desire and a silent promise for a forever future.

BLACK MAGIC RISING

Wilde Witches – Book 1

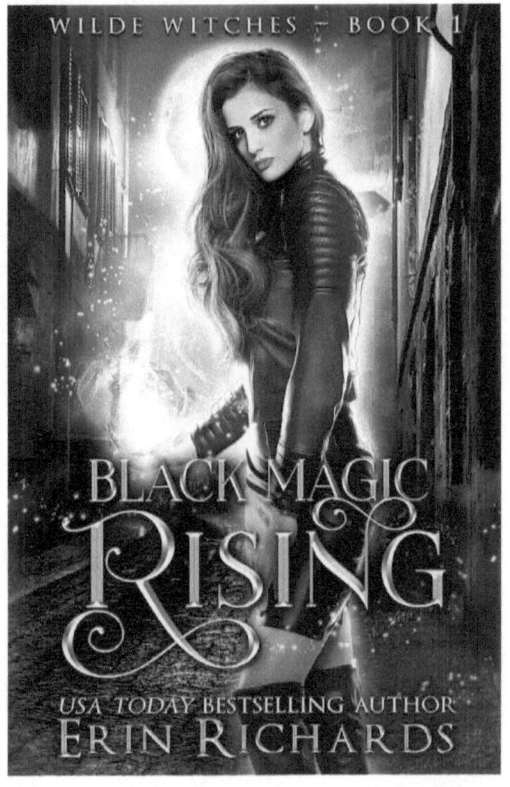

Read Willow Wilde and Evan Ravenwood's story in *Black Magic Rising,* Book 1 of the Wilde Witches series.

ABOUT THE AUTHOR

After lamenting the lack of young adult books to read, award-winning and *USA Today* best-selling author, Erin Richards, wrote her first novel at the age of eighteen hoping to shift the tide. But the only tide she shifted was moving from high school to college. Then everyday life took its toll on her writerly dreams until she couldn't ignore the writing bug any longer. By then, she had immersed herself in reading adult fantasy and romance novels. Writing suspenseful paranormal and fantasy romance was a no brainer and she went on to publish two adult romance novels and hasn't stopped since. But her muse wanted to give that YA writing gig another chance, and Erin finally realized her lifelong dream of publishing a YA novel with the debut of *Vigilante Nights*.

Erin lives in California. In her spare time, she enjoys reading (of course!) and perpetually landscaping her yards, even though she hates digging holes...unless she's burying fictional bodies! She also confesses to a fascination with American muscle cars... and reality TV shows!

Visit Erin Richards online at:
www.erinrichards.com

Sign-up for her newsletter at:
www.erinrichards.com/connect.htm

www.ingramcontent.com/pod-product-compliance
Lightning Source LLC
Chambersburg PA
CBHW032156190626
46808CB00021B/1102